Melanin Romance Presents

Dangerously in Love

Dangerously in Love

BY CHARLENE WORKMAN

DANGEROUSLY IN LOVE

iSeebookz Publishing LLC
Dept: Melanin Romance
Suite137B Commerce Ave Ste 300
 LaGrange GA. 30241

Thank you for your support

Editor: Nicole Dixon.
Cover layout and design by Cheryl Litton & Y.D. Rowland
Cover images Adobe Stock Photos and Unsplash images

ISBN: 979-8-9854863-2-2

Printed in the United States of America

First edition
10 9 8 7 6 5 4 3 2 1

This is a work of fiction; names, characters, places, and incidents are the product of the author's imagination and are fictitiously created and used. Any resemblance to events, locations, or actual persons living or dead is entirely coincidental.

Acknowledgements

A huge thank you! My First thank you to Jesus for allowing me to find a purpose. I prayed and cried to you so much about what my calling is or what can I do while on this earth? You gave me this passion to be a writer. Thank you, father, for not giving up on me. To my family, grandparents, uncles, aunts, nephews and nieces, and cousins, thank you for the love and support you guys have given me. Thank you to my publisher and her team. I appreciate you all believing in me and giving me this opportunity. I'm still amazed that I wrote a book. I can't believe it!

Prologue

"Erick! Wake up, baby, Erick, please, wake up!"

Oh my God, what have I done?

"Baby, I'm so sorry," I said as I sat and watched Erick's lifeless body on my bedroom floor.

The woman he had in my bedroom was screaming and holding her right breast, putting pressure on the gunshot wound. I tried to conduct C.P.R. on Erick, but I knew there wasn't any hope; I knew he was dead. I killed my man. I heard the sounds of police sirens, and an ambulance was coming down the path to my complex; *oh fuck, who called the police?*

(LET ME START FROM THE BEGINNING...) REWIND....

PART ONE
The Beginning

Chapter One

Melinda Stone is my name. I'm a successful lawyer at my father's law firm. My father, Mr. Maxwell Stone, is the H.N.I.C. of his law firm after 60 years in the making. Now he wants to turn the firm over to me.

But I want something different. I feel like I have another calling somewhere else, and staying in the law firm, wasn't it.

But how could I explain this to my father? I'm sitting here with my girls at our favorite restaurant, wanting their professional opinion. I knew I was in for a judgmental conversation.

"YOU GONNA DO WHAT!?" My best friend, Pamela Tucker, yelled out, and everyone in the restaurant stopped their conversations to see what was going on at our table.

"Keep your voice down, girl; Damn," I said, looking around. Since elementary school, Pamela has been my best friend, so her opinion is more important than the other girls. She is also a lawyer at my father's law firm and is very good at what she does. Like many cases I've done, before entering the court, I always stop by her office for prep, and Pamela made sure that my notes and the documents were bang on.

"Girl, you're crazy as hell if you want to step out of your father's law firm and do something different. That's what's wrong with you spoiled rich kids; you got a silver spoon in your mouth and don't know how to use it," said Tasha Campbell rolling her eyes.

"Whatever," I said.

Tasha Campbell and I bumped heads so many times in our childhood days that I never knew we would still hang out as adults.

"You ALL NEED JESUS," said Sasha Morgan.

This bitch thinks since she gave her life to Christ and married a preacher's kid, that now she is holier than us, but before Sasha got married, she was a stripper at Big Cheeky, and her stage name was Passion. The men loved her; Sasha was good at her job and made mad money. Shit, rumor has it she still stops by Big Cheeky from time to time without letting hubby know, but I won't dip into that hot oil right now.

"You know what?" I said, "Let's end this conversation, finish our meals and get the hell outta here." I called the waiter over to drop off the check so we could pay and leave.

Before I headed home, I decided to stop by my parents' house and discuss the situation with my father. I entered my parents' home and was greeted by the sweet smell of my mother's famous peach cobbler. As I tried to grab a bowl from the cabinet, my mother quickly grabbed the bowl out of my hand.

"Damn, ma." I said, "What's your problem?"

"Damn, ma, so you cussing at me now?" She said, looking at me like I was crazy.

"I'm sorry, ma," I said to keep the peace.

My mother and I never had the best relationship. She hated me while giving birth to me. She actually cheated on my father; her affair and scandalous ways created me. Well, my biological father, I don't know who that mutha-fucker is anyway. Mr. Stone raised me as his daughter, and I'm so thankful. From what I gathered; my mother cheated because Maxwell was always into his work. He wanted to make his name have a considerable impact so he didn't have to worry about anything when he retired. So, all my mom had to do was take care of the home. She did, but a woman has needs, and my father wasn't around to provide. So, she ended up booking a suite and traveling to the Virgin Islands for a *me, myself, and I trip;* that's when she bumped into a man named Otis Peterson. Their affair lasted through my mom's whole trip. You see, Otis Peterson was a married man during the trip. He was out on business while his wife was fighting cancer and saw himself becoming a widow. He felt lonely like my mother, and when my mother and Mr. Peterson met, the fling started; but soon after the trip, his wife beat cancer.

Time passed, and my mother found out she was pregnant; of course, she had to tell my father. Maxwell wasn't stupid at all. He did the math and realized the dates didn't add up to my birth. So, Maxwell filed for divorce but remembered my mom had no place to go, so once the divorce was final, he moved her into the guest room down the hall of their home. My parents had a son together before I was born. I say had because my brother is in a nuthouse.

Devin Stone was different from my father. Devin was a player, always in trouble, and my father always bailed him out. One night, Devin went to a club and was greeted by a woman he used to smash. But little did he know, this chick didn't take breakups easy. She purchased him a drink, and this bitch drugged my brother. Early that morning, my father went outside to get the morning newspaper and saw my brother's butt-ass naked, rolling on his lawn like it was winter, rolling in the snow.

They rushed my brother to the hospital. The doctor who examined my brother informed my parents that in his years of practicing medicine, there was no way in hell Devin could or would recover from the voodoo or mumbo jumbo spell (of the drugs). The doctor suggested that my parents put my brother in a facility to get the care he would need. My mother didn't want to say goodbye to her son, but hell, Devin didn't know who anyone was anymore. My mother blamed my father for not spending more time with his son when he was younger, but my father did all he could. He wanted his son to take over the law firm, but my brother made so many mistakes that my father didn't want his name and what he accomplished to burn into flames. So, after putting my brother in the nuthouse, my mother took her trip to the Virgin Islands and met Otis Peterson.

I was 4yrs old, and I remember going with my mother to a store. I was surprised when she saw a man and ran to catch up with him with so much force. It was Otis Peterson. My mother caught up with Mr. Peterson and told him she got pregnant. She introduced me to him. With no hug or a hello, he instantly told my mother to stay the hell away from him and that he was happy with his wife and their children. He told my mother not to bother contacting him again. As I looked up at my mother, I saw her eyes filling with tears. She stood there frozen as the man named Otis Peterson vanished into the crowd of people. I don't know why my mother even bothered trying to find him; hell, Maxwell signed my birth certificate and raised me as his little girl. As I grabbed my mom's hand, she snatched it away and slapped me on my face; ever since then, the hatred for him made her dislike me.

I walked out of the kitchen to avoid a fight with my mother. I went upstairs to my father's study room, where I knew he would be. I tapped on the door and heard a deep man's voice say, "Come in."

"Hey daddy, how are you? I walked to my father's desk and gave him a big hug and kiss on his cheek.

"Hello, my baby girl." My dad embraced me with a hug and kissed me back on my cheek.

"What a surprise to see you today. I thought you would be busy writing your speech to the other partners and me about how you'd make a wonderful lawyer in my absence of retirement."

"Well... dad," I bit my bottom lip gently. "About that," I

said as he lifted his brows and took off his glasses.

"About what, Melinda?"

I took a deep breath. "I think I have another calling beyond being a lawyer, daddy."

I could tell from the look in my father's eyes he was angry that I had just mentioned to him that I didn't want to take his place as the top lawyer of his firm.

"Daddy, listen if you could hear me out," before I could speak, he interrupted me.

"Melinda, do you know what you want to do? What is this calling that you just stop wanting to be a lawyer?

"Well, daddy, not exactly, but I know it's something great."

"Okay, Melinda," and with a look of love, my dad said, "It's your life. Do whatever you want."

I embraced my father with another hug and kiss. And as I walked to the door, my father called, "Melinda."

"Yes, daddy?"

"Make sure you make the smart decision."

"I will, daddy."

I drove home with a smile; glad I didn't take my girlfriend's advice and spoke with my father about what was on my mind. I entered my fabulous three-bedroom, two-and-a-half-bathroom complex with huge windows, where I could see the beautiful view of buildings. Only I lived in the complex, but I loved the space, and the view was gorgeous at night. I wanted to chill and watch a good movie on tv, but my girls wanted to go out to the bar. Pamela, who stayed one floor down from me, entered my home demanding I get ready. I forgot I gave this bitch a key.

"Damn, Pamela, I'm tired as hell. I don't feel like going out tonight." I cried.

"Come on, girl, it will be fun; besides, it's ladies' night. Sasha and Tasha will meet us there."

"Fine." I went to my bedroom and looked at all my clothes in the closet. I chose a cute red dress with a gold belt and wore my red and gold pumps. I let down my curly brown hair, added my make-up, put on a dab of my favorite Japanese blossom perfume, and was ready to go.

"Damn girl," Pamela said, "You look amazing, and that dress makes your ass pop and your curves look stunning."

"Thanks girl, let's go."

***

The parking lot was packed. I didn't think we would ever find a parking space. Once we entered the bar, Pamela and I spotted the girls; as Tasha's ghetto ass kept screaming our names and waving her hands in the air until we saw her. The club's music was banging. The waiter came over to our table and took our drink orders. As we all sat there bobbing our heads to the music, my eyes spotted the door, and walking in was this tall, muscular-built man.

"Damn," I mumbled under my breath. I cleared my throat and told my girls that I'd be back. I'm going to the ladies' room.

Tasha instantly jumps her big ass up, shouting, "I'm coming with you girl." *Fuck, why* I wanted to say.

We walked to the ladies' room. I motioned Tasha to walk in front of me. From the corner of my eyes, I noticed the muscular built man looking me up and down as I walked past him to the restroom.

I fixed my hair and make-up and added a little gloss to my lips. Then, as I was leaving out, some rude bitch bumped into me.

"Damn, excuse you," she rolled her eyes and walked into the restroom.

As I was about to head to the table with my girls, I felt someone grab my arm, pulling me near them. The smell of the cologne turned me on.

"Can I buy you another drink?" He whispered in my ear. I turned around, and here I was, looking at this delicious man right in front of me.

"Sure, you can buy me a drink."

He motioned for the bartender to come our way and

purchased me a glass of red wine. He offered me a seat next to him, and before I could sit down, the same bitch who bumped into me in the bathroom came from nowhere, snapping and making a total fool of herself.

"EEEERRIIICCCCKKK! so you don't see me standing here?" she screeched. "Every time I leave your side, here you go talking to another bitch." She continued.

I got your bitch as I wanted to pop her one good time across her face. Instead, she grabbed an empty bottle out of nowhere and hit it across his face. WHAT THE FUCK. Erick's head dropped onto the counter. The bartender went to the phone, and I knew he was calling for backup. Two king Kong dudes came running to where we were. Erick stepped in front of us and told the security guards to put this raggedy bitch in a cab. He took out his wallet and gave him a hundred-dollar bill. As both men pulled the girl out of the club, I could still hear her yelling, "This won't be the last time you see me, Erick! You better watch your back."

Looking at Erick, "Whoa," I said, "So is that a crazy girlfriend of yours?" I turned and asked the bartender for a napkin cloth and some ice.

"Let me take you to the hospital," I replied.

"Don't be silly," Erick said. "I'll be fine."

"But your lip needs stitches."

He snatched the cloth from me with the ice, and he repeated, "I said I'll be fine."

"Okay," I said.

Noticing that the club was about to close, I saw my girls and I was about to leave Erick until he stopped me in my tracks. He still wanted to have a conversation with me.

My girls were noticing me....

Pamela replied that she would let Tasha and Sasha drive her home and to call her once I got home to make sure I made it safely.

Erick was by my side as I walked to my car; "So miss.... I didn't get your name."

"Oh, I'm sorry. I'm Melinda."

"Melinda Stone, The Melinda Stone at Maxwell law firm that Melinda Stone?" He proclaimed exaggeratedly.

I laughed, "Well, don't be so surprised."

He gently took my hand and kissed it softly." I don't believe it," he said.

After releasing my hand, I opened my handbag and took one of my cards out, and Erick reached for the side of his pants. I instantly saw the gun on his side.

"Whoa," I said as I raised both my hands.

"Relax, boo; this is for the good guys."

Confused by his statement, I corrected him, "You mean the bad guys, right?"

He chuckled, "I am the bad guy."

Erick retrieved his phone, and from the corner of my eyes, I couldn't believe this fool had the nerve to google me to see if I was telling the truth.

Once he found what he was looking for and realized I was telling the truth, I wanted to say *boom* in my Missy Elliott voice. *Open your mouth, give you a taste, hollllaaaa.*

But I kept it classy. "So, you found what you were looking for," I gave him a smirk.

He cleared his throat. "Sorry, I had to make sure. I'm Erick Tyson."

Not acknowledging his name, "Well, it's getting late. I should be going," turning to go, he stopped me in my tracks.

"The night is still young, and I still want to get to know you."

Concerned, I told him. "You need to go to the hospital for those stitches."

"I'm fine; let me take you somewhere nice." He asked. *What could be nice at this time of night;* I thought and looked at my phone; it was 1am. I wanted to say no, but his eyes hypnotized me. *Damn, I couldn't say no to him.*

"I'll follow you," I said.

I was about to open my car door when Erick stood in front of it, looking at me hypnotically. "We are riding in my truck."

We walked for hours (what seemed like hours) till we got to the end of the parking lot to a huge truck. *Damn, how the fuck am I supposed to get in this,* I thought. Erick helped me up into his truck. The inside was breathtaking with leather seats, a fresh car scent, G.P.S., a backup camera, lights under the seats, and huge speakers under the truck. In my mind, I wanted to ask what he did for a living, but I kept it to myself.

We drove to a dark alley, a place I had never driven to in my entire life. I was afraid to even step out.

"Are we going to be safe?"

"Relax," Erick said, "I got you safe with me."

I clung to Erick's arm as we entered a building that I thought was abandoned. Erick opened an odd-looking gate that I had never seen before. But, to my surprise, it was an elevator. As we went up, I heard music; the gate stopped. Erick lifted it up and escorted me out. He held my hand as we entered the door where the loud music was jamming.

Erick must have been to this place a lot; he was so popular. People were giving him high fives; even the DJ announced his name on the mic.

"Oh, shit, MR. TROUBLE IN THE HOUSE, ERICK WAZZUP MAN, " said the DJ.

"Wow, so you must come here often," I said.

Erick looked out into the crowd, "This is my people, you on my block now; I know it's different from you rich folks, but there is a place called middle and poor people class."

Erick walked me to a table in the back. He waved for a lady to come over. I didn't know if this chick worked here or if Erick knew her.

While chewing on what was a massive piece of bubble gum, she came over and said, "Hello, I'm Felicia; what can I get you two tonight?" She blew a giant bubble with the gum that went POP. Erick told the girl to bring a glass of red wine for me and a Heineken for him.

"Be right back," said Felicia as she blew another bubble from her gum, and as she walked away, you heard a POP.

I held in my laugh, but Erick glanced my way and said, "What's so funny?"

"Huh?" I said.

"What's so funny?" he asked as he caressed my arm. I wanted to think of a lie, but I was clueless, so I came out and said it.

"Don't you think you should hate Heineken right now since that was the bottle your thot at the club clucked your face with?" Before Erick could say anything back, Felicia came back with our drinks.

"Here you go, enjoy."

I saw Erick take hold of the bottle, and he chugged down the beverage. His Adam's Apple was moving up and down; *he could drain a bitch pussy by the way he was drinking his beer.*

"How's your wine?" I heard him ask as he placed the empty bottle down. I forgot my wine while I watched him chug down his beverage. I didn't bother taking a sip from the glass. The DJ played some good ass music, and everybody was on the dance floor dancing.

"Time for a slow jam," the DJ called out as he played Joe- I wanna know. *Oh my god, this is my song. I could be in my bathroom playing Joe and letting my shower head do the talking right now.* But instead, Erick interrupted my hard thinking and asked if I wanted to dance.

We entered the dance floor, and he pulled me closer to him; his muscular body was so warm. The scent of his cologne had my panties soaked. I felt his dick brushing on my pussy. If he wanted to, he could have lifted up my skirt right on the dance floor and fuck the hell outta me.

I felt his warm breath on my ear as he rocked my body from side to side. My favorite part of Joe came on "tell me what I gotta do to please you baby, anything you say I do." Erick lifted my chin, and I glanced into his sexy eyes. Erick kissed me softly on my lips, and before I knew it, his tongue was down my throat. The sound of my moaning and how I dug my fingernails in the middle of his back turned Erick on. As I pushed him away for air, he asked if I was ready to go. I nodded yes. We went back to the table. Erick took out another hundred dollars and placed it on the table.

"Let's go," he said.

We went back to the elevator and out to his truck. I looked at my watch; it was almost 4:30 am!

"Erick, I've got to go. I have to be at work in a few hours."

"Relax. I enjoy being with you", and he kissed my fingertips softly.

Before pulling off in his truck, Erick pulled me closer to him and kissed me again. As I caressed my fingers through his curly hair, Erick rubbed on my left leg; the next thing I knew, my legs were wide open as he placed his finger on my pussy and started rubbing my clit. I was so wet, and my body wanted to feel more of Erick.

Erick took me back to his place. Erick was tonguing me down again before we could make it out of the truck. I just wanted him to fuck me right there in the parking lot. My pussy wanted his touch so bad. We walked into his apartment, it was messy as fuck, but that didn't change my mind about wanting him to fuck my brains out. Erick took me to his bedroom, unzipped my dress, and pushed me onto the bed; next, my legs were on his shoulder. Erick's tongue was so thick, long, and warm. Erick was eating my pussy like I was his last supper. My moans became louder, and the more I moved from his lips, the more he pulled me closer to him. I swear I came about eight times. Finally, Erick lifted his face from my legs, and in the moonlight, I could see his face was glistening like a glazed doughnut with my juices all over his face.

I don't know if Erick put on a condom or not. I was so tight, but Erick took his time. My moans got loud, and Erick's dick was so thick I didn't know if my pussy could take all of him. After a couple of minutes, Erick stopped taking his time and proceeded to pound my pussy harder and harder. My moans cried out for help, but I couldn't say the word stop. He felt so damn good as he lifted my legs and spread them farther apart.

"Erick... Erick... Erick," I screamed his name out. My fingernails dug deeper into his back as he kept pounding harder on my pussy. I could hear the sound of my juices as Erick was all in my gut. My pussy was having a concert on his dick; it sounded like cake mix batter when you use a nice metal whisk, stirring all the ingredients to make sure it mixed all together. Erick whispered in my ear to tell me to turn over. He lifted my ass and had me arch my back; he wanted to fuck me doggy style. With all the pounding being done to my pussy, when Erick inserted his dick back inside me, it didn't hurt that much. Erick held onto my waist, and each time I moved forward, he held on to my waist and pulled me back. Each long stroke felt so good.

"Yes, baby, give it to me!" I said.

"You're enjoying this dick?" Erick said.

"Yes, baby, I - I - I am enjoying it!" I screamed out. Smack! Erick slapped my left cheek. Smack! Erick slapped my right cheek.

Over and over again, Erick smacked my ass. As the smacking of his hands on my ass stung, I continued fucking him. Erick grabbed a handful of my hair and pulled my head back; as he kissed me with his tongue exploring down my throat, his dick went deeper, faster, and harder, and he continued to fuck me so good. This was the best dick I ever had in my entire life. Finally, Erick released my hair and raised himself on the bed. Oh shit, he's standing up in it. As the full moon glistened, lighting up the bedroom.

My legs were shaking, and Erick was breathing heavily. He laid on his back as I said to myself, *It's over. My pussy can't take NO more.* Eric, breathing heavily, spoke and said, "Get on top."

"WHAT!?"

"Get on top babe. Are you scared?" he chuckled.

I thought to myself, *my pussy won't function right by the time the night is over*. I climbed on top of Erick and gently ground my swollen clit on his stiff dick. Erick was getting a little aggravated. He lifted my hips a little and slammed my pussy on his dick.

I bit my bottom lip so hard that the pain matched my swollen, throbbing pussy. I was surprised that my body was still moist. I really thought Erick drained me out. I tried to get enough strength to blow Erick's brains out as he grabbed my breast and sucked gently on my nipples. I fucked Erick so good that, the moment came, and he finally busted his release inside me. The warmth of his semen trickled down my legs. I realized I had to go to the bathroom, but being dick down was so good; there's no way in hell I was about to pee.

My clit was throbbing hard at the same rate as my heartbeat. Erick pulled me close to him, and before closing my eyes to sleep, he whispered into my ear and told me I was now his woman. As I smiled and closed my eyes, I realized I was Erick's girl, and he was my man.

Chapter Two

The loud noise of a car horn startled my sleep as I looked over at the clock on the nightstand. It was 7:30 am.

"Oh shit, I'm going to be late!" I yelled.

I woke up Erick to the sound of me running around trying to put on my clothes.

"Erick! Get up. We gotta go! Get up!" I yelled.

As he rubbed his eyes and stretched with a loud yawn, "Go where Melinda?"

"My car, I have to get to my car. Remember I rode with you? My car is still at the bar, which I hope it is. Come on. I got to get to my office asap." I told him.

"Oh, shit yeah," Erick said, stumbling quickly to put on his clothes and shoes. I lost sight of seeing Erick's massive dick in broad daylight. It was a wonder with all the fucking we did throughout the night; it was still stiff and damn long and thick.

"Are you ready?" Erick said.

"Yeah yeah, I'm ready." I put on my heels, but was still looking around for my underwear. Fuck it, I don't need it anyway, I thought; my clit is still swollen.

We finally made it to my car. Thank God it was still in excellent condition. As I got out of Erick's truck, he grabbed my arm and said, so you are not going to give me a kiss? I smiled and kissed him before it became passionate. I told him I had to go. I'll call you later, he said. I waved bye and got into my car. It was now 8:15 am. I didn't have time to rush home, shower, and dress, but I could in my office. I'm a daddy's girl, and my father spoiled me; upon request, I had my office customized with a full bathroom. I sped down the road to the law firm and parked in my parking spot. I rushed up the stairs onto the elevator and pressed the 7th-floor button. As I waited for the doors to open, I saw my reflection on the elevator doors. I looked like a mess, but it was worth it. The doors finally opened. I tried to rush quickly to my office and pass my assistant Donna before she could tell me anything. I ran straight into my office, closed the door, and breathed a sigh of relief.

"Well, well, well, you're alive," said the voice behind me. It was Pamela. I jumped quickly.

"Jesus! Pam, you scared me."

"I went by your place, and you weren't there, nor was your car. Were you out with that dude all night Melinda?" Pamela said, annoyed.

"Look, Pammie," I called her by the nickname I used to call her in college. "I had too much to drink, and he didn't want me to drive home. Sorry I didn't call you Pammie."

She knew I was lying. Pamela knows me better than I know myself.

" Yeah, right, Melinda, I'm not dumb. I can smell him all over you, and you look like a hot ass mess."

"I can't have this conversation with you, Pammie. I have a client that will be here in a few minutes. Will you please let me take a shower and get ready? "

"Fine, whatever," Pamela said. She left my office. I got myself together, looking like the lawyer I should be. I prepared my notes and waited for my client.

***

After my meeting at work, the girls and I went to a nice dinner. I thought my situation at the bar the other night was totally forgotten. I was wrong. It was the topic of the hour.

"Where did you and this guy end up going?" Tasha asked.

"Why do I have to tell you, my business?" I asked them.

"We were worried sick about you, girl," said Sasha. "I prayed and prayed and asked God to guide you to be safe wherever you were. We are your girls, like sisters, and you just left with some stranger." Sasha was getting on my last nerves.

"Sasha, I don't need your shit right now." We fussed back and forth; Sasha was pissing me off.

"You need Jesus to ask God to forgive you and cleanse you of your sins."

I gave Sasha the finger instead of cursing her out. She knew what I meant. She reached into her blouse and pulled out her cross necklace, shaking it at me like I was a damn demon or something. We all laughed.

I explained to the girls where Erick had taken me and that I had a great time. Then, out of the blue, Sasha asked, "Did you fuck him?"

"NO!" I said. I looked at Pamela, and in her eyes, she knew I was lying.

***

I got home, and just as promised, Erick called me, telling me how much he missed me and wanted to see me again.

"I miss you too," I said.

"So, when are you going to invite me over to your place?" He asked. Without thinking, I asked him when he wanted to come over. He responded by saying tomorrow night. Being clueless, I thought he would say either next week or whenever I'm ready, but tomorrow night?

I had no plans; however, I wanted to rest since it was Friday, and I wanted a weekend of sleep and relaxation.

"Hello Melinda, is tomorrow night okay for you?"

"Yeah, yeah, tomorrow night is fine. Can't wait to see you," I responded.

I got prepared for bed and texted Pamela, apologizing for my behavior at the office. She responded with an apology for intruding. She just wanted me to be safe. I told her I loved her and sent her a kissy face emoji. Laying in my bed, I held tightly to my pillow, wishing it was Erick's body I was lying on. I finally fell asleep and slept till 3 pm. Man, I was exhausted. I didn't even hear my phone buzzing on my nightstand. Six missed calls from Erick and 12 unread messages from Erick, my father, and my assistant Donna. Before I could get myself together and get out of bed, my phone rang; it was Erick.

"Yes, boo," I answered.

"Damn, woman, you can't answer your phone. A nigga was worry sick bout you."

"I'm sorry, hun. I was exhausted and needed a few extra hours of sleep." I told him.

Erick's tone of voice made me a little uncomfortable, but I didn't take it to heart. My baby was just concerned about me.

"So, what's on the menu?" he said.

"What do you mean?" I asked.

"Food woman, remember I'm coming over tonight."

Damn, he wants me to cook. "I'll prepare something special for you, baby," I promise.

"Okay, good because a nigga hungry, and you already

know what I want afterward for dessert." He replied with laughter in his voice. I gave a sexy laugh.

"Oh yeah, what is that?"

He laughed and told me that I would find out. "Text me your address, babe. I got to handle some business, and when I'm done, I'll be headed to see you."

Before I could say anything, Erick hung up the phone. *Damn, I wish my mother would've taught me how to cook. Instead, take-out is my go-to for everything.* I looked into my cabinet and freezer to see what I had. I was hopeless. I called up Pamela to see if she could help me.

"Pammie, I need you asap. I'm trying to prepare a special dinner."

Pamela interrupted me, "Melinda cooking?"

"Yes, Pammie, I'm cooking." Even though I knew she couldn't see me, I rolled my eyes.

"Is it for this Erick dude?" she interrupted again.

I breathed heavily on the phone; "Are you going to help me or not?" I finished.

"I will be there in a minute," said Pamela.

Pamela opened the door to my complex as I was in the kitchen. "What are you doing?" she asked as the burnt smoke lingered in the air.

Pamela held a baking pan and a brown paper bag, which she placed on the table.

"Here, this is seasoned chicken with peppers and onions. I'll start making your rice and veggies," she said while laughing.

"Oh, thank you, Pammie." I gave her a big hug.

"I still think you need to look into this guy's background Melinda; I don't want you to get hurt."

"Pamela, he cares so much about me. He is a good man, and I'm happy."

"If you say so," said Pamela.

Pamela left after the meal was finished, and I waited for Erick to arrive. Finally, at 9:00 pm, Erick knocked on my door.

"This is nice, boo," said Erick.

"Thanks," I said as I held his hand and walked him to the table displaying the food that Pamela had prepared.

He smiled, "Damn boo, you made all this?"

"Of course, baby, I made this meal just for you." I kiss him on his lips. Erick tongued me down so good that my pussy throbbed inside my shorts.

As I gasp for air, "Baby, let's eat before dinner gets cold."

We ate dinner, and I knew I was the dessert. Erick had me pinned down on my island countertop in the kitchen. Just like before, he ate my pussy, but this time, his long thick fingers were rubbing my clit in a circular motion. As he placed two fingers inside my pussy I cooed. I was still sore from the night at Erick's apartment, but I enjoyed Erick's touch. As his fingers went in and out, my pussy and his saliva trickled down my pussy. Finally, I grabbed Erick's hand and pulled him up to kiss me. I kissed and sucked on his tongue, tasting my sweet passion off his lips. Then, I heard Erick unzip his pants, and he instantly inserted his massive dick inside me. I clung to the side of the countertop as Erick pounded his dick in and out of me.

Something must have really bothered my man as he kept pounding his dick inside me with so much force. Finally, the pain was so much to bear that I asked Erick to stop as I pushed his chest back to break free. But instead, he grabbed hold of my hand and placed it above my head.

"Erick, baby, please, I can't take anymore," I begged.

I felt like my walls were about to rip as I was so sore that I probably had to decline if Erick wanted more of me again. Finally, Erick burst his warm nectar all inside my swollen pussy. My legs were so weak I couldn't even get off the countertop. Erick lifted my tired body off the counter and walked to my bedroom as he ran a hot bath for me to soak my sore body.

The hot water that touched my aching clit stung so bad. But I sat there and watched the steam. Finally, I closed my eyes, only to wake up to hear Erick's loud voice cussing someone out on the phone. I wrapped myself in a long towel and opened the bathroom door. Erick was sitting on the edge of my bed as I rubbed his back; he pushed me hard so that my back hit my headboard.

Once he got off the phone, he snapped, "Listen, when I'm on the phone bitch don't bother me!"

"Bitch! Excuse me?" I yelled. *No, this muthafucker didn't just call me a bitch.*

"Baby, I'm sorry," he said as he kissed my forehead. He was so tense, and I thought maybe I shouldn't have bothered him while on the phone.

"Apology accepted," I said.

"Look, I got to head out, but I'll talk to you later," Erick said. He gave me a peck on the lips and left.

***

Erick met up with the yellow bone chick that busted his lip at the bar around the corner from my complex. When she opened the door to his truck and got in, she slapped him.

"You were with that Bitch weren't you, Erick?" She said accusingly.

"Listen, Bitch!" Erick grabbed his gun from his side compartment and held it against her head. "Let's stick to the plan as we promised. Now, I want to take the whole family out for my brother's death; if you stuck to what I told you, we wouldn't have an issue now, would we? And if Kitty would have given Devin Stone the right amount of dosage in his drink, he'd be six feet under by now, but since his stupid ass don't know a damn thing and is in the nuthouse, I'll leave it at that." Erick continued.

Scared and panicking that her life would be over, the girl responded with tears running down her face. "Yes, I-I-I'll stick to the plan please, Erick, don't kill me."

Erick laughed and lowered the gun from the side of her face. "Get out my damn truck and be at my apartment tonight so I can beat that pussy to a pulp."

***

I woke up to Pamela at my bedroom door. "Geesh, girl, what the fuck?!" I said while I grabbed my sheets to cover my bare-naked body.

"So, where is Erick? He must be one of those hit and quit and leave type of niggas." She said.

"Look, don't talk about my man like that; he left to handle some business," I explained.

"Yeah, right; what type of job does he have, where does he work, how much income does he bring home?"

All the damn questions Pamela was throwing at me, I didn't know the answer. I looked at her dumbfounded and mumbled; I never asked Erick what type of work he does.

Shaking her head. "Basically, you fucking a man you don't know a damn thing about; what's wrong with you,

Melinda? For God's sakes, you are a lawyer. I wonder if Mr. Maxwell knows what his little girl is doing behind closed doors?"

"Leave my father out of this, Pamela. I'm a grown-ass woman, and what I do inside my house is my fucking business."

"Whatever," said Pamela, "you know what, Melinda, you have changed since meeting this Erick guy." And she walked out of my bedroom and left.

***

Early one morning, I woke up refreshed and prepared for work. I decided to put on my navy-blue pants suit and six-inch pumps. I put my curly hair in a messy bun and went out my apartment door to the elevator. In the parking, I remotely unlocked my car. As I placed my purse inside my vehicle, I saw who appeared to be the same yellow chick that called me a bitch at the club. As I wanted to pop her ass on her lip for calling me a bitch and for hitting my man with a damn bottle. I checked the time and realized I was late for work; she was so lucky as I thought *I'd deal with her later.*

While driving to work, I was startled by the ringing of my phone; it was my father.

"Good morning, daddy; how are you?"

"Morning, baby girl, you must be on your way to work."

"Yes, daddy, I am. Is there something you need me to do for you when I get there?"

"Now that you mentioned it, my father said, I need you and Pamela to come together for this important project. You must do this as a team."

"Daddy Pamela and I aren't on talking terms right now; my father cut me off as I tried to explain.

"Melinda, put the differences aside and complete this project for me. This is for the company, please."

"Okay daddy, I will."

"Thanks baby girl; I love you."

"Love you too, daddy."

"Ms. Stone," said Donna when I arrived.

"What Donna, what is it? Can I settle into my office before you start letting me know what's on my agenda today?" I said, exasperated.

"Yes, ma'am, but you have five messages from a Mr. Johnathon Cane," she stated.

Today is not the damn day for this shit. I was thinking to myself. Johnathon Cane is also a lawyer; his company is not as successful as my father's firm. He has been trying to run my father's hard work to the ground but lost all the time. Mr. Cane wanted to buy my father's company for so many years, and my father turned him down. Now that my father is about to retire, he is coming after me in an attempt to buy the company. As I took the notes out of Donna's hand, she wasn't finished with me.

"One more thing Ms. Stone," as she cleared her throat.

"We at Maxwell law firm are so proud and blessed for your father's hard work, and we will miss him so much. We agreed that you and Ms. Pamela Tucker should handle his retirement party." Donna declared.

"Seriously!?" I yelled. I walked to my office and closed the door hard.

I had a terrible headache and wanted to go back home, curl up in bed, and sleep. Instead, I checked my cell phone and realized I hadn't spoken with Erick in two weeks. I hope my man is okay. A knock sounded at my door as I tried to start my day. Pamela walked into my office, announcing, "I just got off the phone with your father, and he wants us both to work on this project."

I buzzed Donna to bring me a hazelnut coffee and bring it fast. Pamela yelled out, bring two, please. Without saying much, I let Pamela take the floor to discuss what we would do with the project. As she talked, my phone started buzzing; it was a text from Erick.
I need to talk to you; it's urgent. So, I replied I would be home around 5 pm, come over then.

***

Pulling up to my complex, I was exhausted. After I got off the elevator, Erick was waiting at my door, looking like a hot mess. He could barely stand up straight, and it looked like he had been drinking. As I opened the door, I managed to help Erick inside.

"Erick, baby, what's wrong with you? Where have you been?"

"I lost it all, boo, I lost it all," he said.

"You lost what, Erick?"

"I lost everything; my home and my business. I have nowhere to go. All I have is my truck."

"Baby, calm down; everything will be okay." Lifting his head in my hands, I smelled the odor of liquor.

"Where have you been, baby? If you want to stay here, you can."

I know Erick, and I haven't been dating that long, but I cared; I loved him, and I couldn't bear the thought of my man on the streets. Erick and I rested peacefully in each other's arms until the following day. I called Donna to inform her I would be working from my desk at home if she needed to call me.

Some time had passed after working from home. As I was writing some final ideas on a notepad for my father's retirement party, Pamela and I were completing I heard Erick's loud voice fussing and cussing at whoever was on the phone.

I walked into the kitchen to prepare myself a hot cup of hazelnut coffee. When I turned from the counter, Smack! Erick hit me across my face. "Bitch, didn't you hear me calling you?" Erick yelled. Grabbing a handful of my hair Erick dragged me across the floor. I didn't know what possessed Erick. What type of monster had he become?

As fast as his temper had flared, Erick apologized, "Baby, I'm so sorry I don't know what came over me. Please forgive me, boo," as he kissed my swollen cheek.

Later that afternoon...I stood still in the mirror and saw what Erick had done. I tried to put more makeup on my face. I didn't want the girls to see the red mark of Erick's handprint on my cheeks. The girls and I had a quick brunch as I sat quietly, listening to everyone talk. They knew something was up and was concerned about my silence as I am never silent around them, not one bit. Pamela couldn't keep her eyes off me and knew something was up, but I didn't have any time to bother with her shit. We still weren't on good terms.

****

One evening after work, a day before my father's big retirement event, I got home to find Erick in the living room watching tv on my flat screen. I placed my purse on the counter, dropped my keys inside the dish, and headed to the bedroom.

"Hey baby, how was your day?"

I ignored what he said and opened the door to my room with a huge surprise waiting on the other side. Beautiful pink roses filled my room. Erick brought a dozen of pretty pink roses. The smell of the roses smelled so sweet. As I was about to walk farther into my bedroom, I got pulled back by Erick's strong arms as he kissed me on my neck.

"I'm sorry, Melinda, baby, do you love your surprise," Erick asked.

I turned around and gave him a peck on his lips. After that, Erick and I made love. Buzz buzz was the sound of Erick's phone on the nightstand. While Erick was sleeping, I quietly took his phone to see who was blowing him up. It was a text message from a woman named Kitty that wanted to be out of the game. She had completed what he wanted from her and now wanted her money. *Who is this bitch Kitty, and what did she complete for Erick? Is Erick cheating on me?* I thought to myself.

ERICK WOKE UP before I could place his phone back on the stand.

"Why the fuck are you going through my phone?"

He yelled blow after blow after blow. Erick continued hitting me as I screamed for him to stop and said, I was sorry, I thought Erick was going to kill me, and Pamela was right; I should have researched Erick.

****

It was the big night of my father's retirement party. Unfortunately, I would not make it as Erick made my face his own punching bag the day before.

I spoke with my father, stating I wouldn't make it to his dinner ceremony. It was his big day to celebrate, for everyone to surprise him at the party both Pamela and I put together. I told him I wasn't feeling well with a stomach ache and needed rest. He understood and told me to take care and feel better. I placed ice on my swollen face, took a pain pill, and crashed into a deep sleep.

"What the fuck happened to your face?" Shouted Pamela as I woke up in shock at her appearance standing in front of me.

"I've been clumsy lately, been tripping over shit."

"You think I'm fucking stupid! Did Erick do this shit to you? Where that mutha fucker at."

"Pammie, please, he-he didn't mean it. He's been going through a lot lately."

"Melinda, that doesn't give him the right to beat you like a damn punching bag. Where the fuck is he" as she checked everywhere in my complex. "ERICK! ERICK! ERICK! You wanna beat somebody, beat my ass."

"Pamela, I yelled; he's not here. Please stop screaming. I have a killer headache. What are you doing here anyway?"

"So, you, trying to change the subject?" Pamela responded. "Well, since you didn't come to your father's retirement party, he told me you weren't feeling well and had me stop by with a few plates of food from the party."

Erick came in, and Pamela started screaming and cursing at him without saying hello.

"Who the fuck gives you the right to put your fucking hands on my sister."

"Bitch get the fuck outta my face before I lay hands on you."

"Do it, please do, and I have your ass locked up, so help me, god."

Erick laughed like Pamela was a damn joke.

"Bitch you think I'm afraid of the damn police. Get the fuck out of my house before I drag you by your weave and throw you the fuck out."

"Please, y'all, stop fighting!" I yelled, "Please stop it!" I ran in between them to break them up.

Erick's last statement pissed Pamela off more.

"Your house nigga! This is Melinda's house. You need to get your shit and get the fuck out and stay away from Melinda."

Erick moved to slap Pamela. I grabbed him by the arm and kindly asked her to go.

"Please, for me, just leave Pammie."

"So, you choose this fool over me? Me? Me! Really Melinda?"

I didn't say anything as tears came down my cheeks.

"Fine," Pamela said. "I hope to see you later if he doesn't have you in a coffin, and the last time I see your face is at your funeral."

Pamela stormed out of my bedroom and slammed the door behind her.

"How the fuck she got in here." Shouted Erick. I was still crying that I chose Erick over my long-time best friend.

"Pamela has a key to my complex."

"I don't like how she disrespects me. That bitch needs to be put in her place, and you need to get your key back or change the damn locks, and that's final," he said as he entered the bathroom to shower.

I took a few of my vacation days to not go to work. While Donna, my assistant, was surprised since working for my father's law firm, I never missed a day of work, let alone been late or called out. I'm good at my job and love what I do. Looking at myself in my vanity mirror, I repeatedly told Donna, yes, I'm taking a few days off. I have the stomach flu. Even if I tried to go to work, it would take more than just make-up to cover the bruises.

"Donna, transfer all my messages to Pamela or someone else at the office. I'll let you know when I am coming back."

I knew Pamela wouldn't say anything to the people at the office or the girls about what happened. She is a true friend. I tried to touch my face with some Vaseline in the mirror. I looked hideous. Was I becoming a weak bitch? Why can't I face Erick and tell him to leave? Or have him make a decision. If he puts his hands on me again, I'm filing for a restraining order? Erick woke up yawning and sat up on the bed.

"Morning, baby, why are you not here next to me?" He patted my side of the bed.

I came and sat next to him. He pulled me in the middle, and instead of doing what he usually does, which was eating my pussy first, he shoved his dick into my wet pussy and fucked the shit out of me. As I sat there getting my pussy smashed, I tried to hold my moans, but Erick's dick was so big and long that I couldn't control my moans. His dick action was good. Erick sucked on my earlobe and placed my left leg on his shoulder, kissing the back of my leg.

"Fuck me, Erick," I blurted out; inch by inch, width by width, his dick pounded my pussy as I kept getting wetter and wetter. Erick kept filling my pussy up with his love. Ultimately, Erick screamed and exploded all inside my walls. As he lay on my chest, breathing heavily on my neck, I looked up at my customized ceiling mirrors. I thought to myself. *I am a weak bitch.*

***

Tasha created a group text and asked us to meet her at a café shop. Everyone agreed to meet up, but I declined, informing them I was under the weather. Both Tasha and Sasha responded if they needed to come over... I quickly answered that I would be fine. At the café, the girls asked Pamela if I was okay since we both lived in the same complex.

"Fuck her," she said.

"What....!?" As both Tasha and Sasha were stunned at Pamela's answer.

"What is going on with you and Melinda? What did we miss?"

"I don't want to talk about it," said Pamela.

Even though Pamela and I had a fallout, her loyalty was still solid

$$\mathcal{C}hapter \; \mathcal{T}hree$$

It had been two weeks since I stepped foot inside the law firm. I was doing much better. My face had healed enough, so nobody would notice what Erick did to me.

"Good morning Ms. Stone; welcome back," said Donna.

"Morning, Donna," I said while I walked, staring at my phone and heading to my office. I stopped at my door and politely asked Donna to call Pamela to stop by my office when she arrived.

"Oh, you didn't hear Ms. Stone?"

"Hear what?" I asked

"Well, Ms. Tucker won't be in all week; she is meeting with Johnathon Cane to make a transfer to leave the firm," Donna explained.

I was shocked and confused after sitting in my car, which seemed like forever. Thinking of the fight at my complex. Did choosing Erick over Pamela cause her to leave the company? And if I decided to take over my father's law firm, Pamela knew and agreed she'd be my right hand. I left the parking lot of my father's firm, and I headed home. Luckily to my surprise, I saw Pammie in her personal parking space. Getting a few bags out of her trunk, *she must have been shopping*, I thought. Then, she vanished into the revolving doors to the elevator. I tried my best to rush into my empty parking space and catch up with her. Running with six-inch pumps was a workout as I caught my breath and asked the person on the other side of the door to hold it for me.

Pamela saw it was me and stated, "Wait for the next one."

But I forced myself in and stood in the corner. As the elevator door closed, I had to tell Pamela how I felt about her leaving and also made an apology. I asked for you at the office today as I kept my head down to the floor. Pamela still wasn't saying anything to me.

"Listen, I'm sorry for how I acted at my complex. I didn't want Erick to hurt you."

"But you allowed him to hurt you. What the fuck Melinda."

"Let me explain, Pamela?"

"There is nothing you can explain. You made your choice; your choice is Erick's controlling ass over me!" She stated as she slapped the palm of her hand on her chest.

"I'm sorry, I miss you, girl. You are my best friend. Hell, we are basically sisters. Pamela, I won't be the same if you want to throw our friendship to the drain."

I can't deal with Tasha and Sasha by myself in the public eye," responded Melinda. Pamela let out a smirk.

"So, are you leaving the firm?" I asked

"I don't know," replied Pamela. "Melinda, you hurt me so much that I couldn't stand to be near you. However, my loyalty stands with your father. He has been so good, and he taught me the ropes.

"I don't want to leave the firm; we are family. Besides, Johnathon Cane is a creep." I said.

"Father Maxwell got him beat," said Pamela.

We slapped high fives and laughed. Unfortunately, we didn't realize the elevator had stopped on Pamela's floor.

"I miss you, girl."

"Miss you too."

As Pamela exited, I had to stop her. "Hey, Pammie, are we still up for the girl trip coming up."

"Hell yeah!" she screamed.

Pamela got off the elevator, and I pushed the button to my floor.

I opened my door and was greeted by a delicious aroma. Erick was in the kitchen cooking.

"Glad you're home." He came over and kissed my lips.

"How 'bout you go take a nice shower, and dinner will be ready when you come out." He spun me around and smacked me on my ass.

The hot water relieved the stress off my body. As I was trying to enjoy my hot shower, a sign came to me. *Erick's been living with me for about three months now and never once stepped into my kitchen to cook anything. Oh fuck*, as I drop the soap in the tub, *he is trying to kill me. Erick is trying to kill me.*

"BABY," Erick tapped on the door. "Are you okay? Dinner is ready."

"I'll be out in a second." I didn't know what to do.

Damn it. My phone was inside my purse on the counter. *Fuck I couldn't call Pamela. Maybe he's trying to apologize for all the pain he caused me and trying to make a change. Maybe Erick wants to do the right thing*, I thought.

I got dressed, put on sweat pants and a t-shirt, and walked into the kitchen. Erick set the table so beautifully. It was a candlelight dinner with a fresh bottle of my favorite wine.

"Well, are you going to sit down," Erick said.

"Of course," I stated.

Erick went out with a bang. He prepared steak and potatoes, butter rolls, and green beans. *Which food has the poison, maybe all of it except for his?* I thought to myself.

"Well, are you going to eat up?" he asked while cutting his steak.

I was hungry but also scared. So, I ate until I couldn't eat anymore. Thinking about how I was feeling, there weren't any symptoms afterward, and I was feeling fine. Erick took my empty plate only to return to start kissing me all over my neck. He turned my chair around and lifted my chin. While I stared into his eyes, he tongue kissed me; I thought, *maybe I'll be his dessert again, perhaps he will eat my pussy on the table?*

Erick unzipped his pants, dropped his boxers, and out came his massive hard dick in my face. "Open wide," he said.

"WHAT?"

"Open your mouth, open your mouth," Erick said repeatedly, and I did what I was told.

Erick eased his dick inch by inch into my mouth. I felt the head of his dick pounding down my throat. I sucked his massive dick as it formed a rhythm in the corner of my mouth. My saliva dripped from the corner of my lips and down my chin. Erick held the back of my head and pushed more of his penis inside my mouth. I had to breathe from my nose. My jaw bone started to get sore, causing pain. I moved Erick's body from me to gasp for air. He grabbed my face, kissed me, and placed his dick back inside my mouth. I took in a mouth full of his dick, and it felt like I was sucking for hours. Finally, Erick let out a heavy moan and released all his cum at the back of my throat. Without taking his dick out of my mouth, Erick looked at me, staring like he was waiting for me to swallow. Choking on the amount of semen, I managed to swallow it down.

Erick took off my sweatpants, bent me over my barstool, and fucked me. I clung, holding on tight to the stool as Erick pounded my pussy to a pulp. Finally, he leaned over, placed my hair to the side, and whispered in my left ear. Are you ready for your next surprise? I nodded yes, and Erick demanded I stay bent over the bar stool. When he returned, I heard Erick unzip something out of a bag. I felt something cold oozing down my ass. Erick massaged the liquid on both of my ass cheeks, gave them a hard smack, and said, relax. My eyes grew BIG. Erick was about to...

I screamed for mercy as Erick's enormous dick entered my tight ass. I have never in my life done anal, and the feeling of doing it with Erick, I didn't enjoy it. Inch by inch, Erick fucked me in my ass. I begged him to stop, but he insisted I be a big girl and take this dick. Finally, Erick nutted again. His cum dripped from my ass and onto my thighs. I laid on the barstool, too weak to even try to stand.

*****

The big day finally arrived, and our girl's trip finally came. As I gather up my suitcase and bags, rushing to make it to the airport and meet up with the girls. Pamela and I decided to take a cab together.

"Are you leaving me already?" Erick sat up on the side of the bed. Looking like a sad puppy dog.

"Good morning to you too, and yes, I told you that every two years, the girls and I would each gather around and plan a trip together. It's a tradition."

"How come I never met your other two girlfriends," Erick asked.

"Tasha, you can meet; she might like you. But, on the other hand, Sasha is almost a preacher's wife, and she would pray for you while blessing you with holy water." I laughed while kissing him on his lips.

"Very funny, I was told I am a sinner child that needs prayer and worship. So maybe Sasha is not bad to meet after all."

"Knock it off," I said and continued to get ready.

Erick got up while I was bent over, putting on my sandals.

"Erick, I'm going to be late."

He didn't know I was 2 hours early, heading to the airport.

"Listen, he said you better not be going on this trip meeting another man and giving him what's mine. You better tell them, lames, you got a nigga at home."

"Are you jealous," I said.

"Don't fucking play with me, Melinda." Erick touched my right cheek with his fingertips. As Erick kissed me, he pushed me on the bed, raised my sundress, pulled my pink satin panties to the side, and ate my pussy.

Enjoying the moment, I questioned how he could be jealous? I still haven't forgotten the girl named Kitty programmed in his phone. Erick ate my pussy well and sucked all my juices.

As he got up, he said, "Giving you something to remember me by."

I look at the clock on my nightstand. Great, I have enough time to meet Pamela. I pushed Erick on the bed and rode him like I was at a Kentucky Derby. My ass bounced up and down, and the sound of Erick's moaning turned me on even more. I watched Erick's face and his reaction from above as I looked in my mirror on my ceiling. He bit his bottom lip and held my waist. I knew my pussy was the shit. After a few more pouncing on Erick, his warm nectar released all inside of me. I look at the time; damn it, I have to go. I left Erick there. Motionless, with his dick empty, lying on his thigh. I would get cleaned up at the airport and left running out of my complex with my bags.

"Hurry up, girl, the cab is here," cried Pamela...

"I'm coming and running as fast as I can!" The moisture of my juices and Erick's semen was sticking to my thighs.

"I thought Erick wouldn't let you go."

"Bitch, please. " I laughed.

"Ain't no man going to tell me I can't come on this trip as much money I paid for my ticket."

"I know that," said Pamela.

We finally pulled up to the airport and spotted Tasha and Sasha.

"Are you girls ready?" they shouted.

We grabbed our bags, tipped the driver, and headed inside. We checked in, entered the airplane, and took our seats, and the flight attendant announced a 20-minute flight delay. So, hold tight, and we will be off soon.

"Okay, ladies, I will be back; I'm going to freshen up in the bathroom."

The plane was ready to take off when I took my seat. I felt refreshed after cleaning myself up. Costa Rica, here we come shouted Tasha as we all cheered. I placed my headset on, listened to the sound of R&B, and closed my eyes.

"Wake up, we're here," said Pamela.

"I can't believe I slept through the whole plane ride."

As we exited, we were greeted with Welcome to Costa Rica, and a tall medium-built man was holding a sign with my name on it. "Girls, this way." I motioned them to follow.

"Are you Melinda Stone," the man asked.

"Yes, I am."

"Right this way, ladies."

He opened the door to a nice long limo. The girls were speechless. What is this? They asked.

"Well, I added a few more dollars and got us a limo and a driver to take us to our suite."

They all screamed in surprise and went inside.

Once at the suite. We were greeted again by the owner, who offered us a glass of champagne. We all thanked him as he welcomed us to Costa Rica. I glanced at the beautiful scenery, warm weather, and people from everywhere having a good time. This is beautiful, I said, and the girls agreed with me.

Thank you, I hope you have a wonderful time here. Please let me introduce myself. My name is Mark Hamilton, and I am the owner of this resort. Let me walk you to the lounge and get you all checked inside. Once we checked into our rooms, the girls and I suggested we meet up later for dinner. So, we all departed to our rooms. I tried calling Erick and telling him I had made it, but there was no response. He must be still sprung and asleep. I laughed.

The view outside my room was breathtaking. The ocean was a clear blue, and the trees blew softly into the wind. I pulled open the patio door allowing the fresh breeze to touch my skin so cool, relaxing, and free. I let my curly hair out of its ponytail, closed my eyes, and listened to the sounds of the people enjoying the time of their lives. I entered my bedroom greeted by a basket of goodies and a card from Mark Hamilton. Mr. Hamilton thanked his guest for choosing his suite and asked if we needed anything to call the front desk. I unpacked my things and was ready to relax and take a soothing bath. I opened a bottle of champagne and watched as the water filled the tub. I tried to call Erick again, but still, no answer.

"Fuck it," I said. This is my vacation. I need this after everything I've been through with Erick; he isn't going to ruin my time here.

***

At my complex, Erick woke up to several missed calls from me, and an unknown number was buzzing his phone line.

"Who the fuck is this?"

"It's me, Erick," said the woman on the other line.

"Oh, wassup, boo."

"I miss you," she replied.

"Oh, you do," he chuckled.

"Well, bring your fine ass here and show me how bad you miss me."

"I'm not coming over to that bitch hou.... " Erick interrupted her.

"Chill, she is not here, she won't be here for two weeks, and we got the whole place to ourselves. We got to sit down and continue with this plan. I'm ready to take her and her bitch ass family out for my brother Silk's sake. I'll text you the address, so be on your way."

***

The girls and I met up at the lounge and went to a nice elegant spot. Sweet music was playing on stage as a band performed lovely music. We waited for an empty table and were seated in the middle section near the bar. We ordered our drinks and reviewed the menu to place our order. As we waited, I saw a group of handsome men entering the doorway. They walked past our table, and one of the men from the group noticed me and politely came my way.

"Are you Melinda Stone?"

"Yes, I am, and you are ....?"

"Oh, excuse me, I'm Sheldon Mitchell."

"Your name doesn't ring a bell to me."

"Oh, I know," he said. "A while back, I had an interview with your father, Maxwell Stone."

"Listen, as I raised my hand to his face, I'm not here to talk about business or my father's law firm. I'm here on vacation with my girls, and we are here to have a good time, right ladies?"

"Yes, that's right."

Sheldon saw the way I looked at him ...

"No, No, it's not like that- I was trying to get a job there, and I guess my resume didn't spark your father's interest, and he turned me down."

"Hmmm, I'm sorry to hear that. My father is a strong, bold man who knows who will be fit to join his branch."

"Yes, I agree," he said.

"Well, my buddies and I are also here on vacation." I turned to where he pointed to a table with delicious yet handsome fine ass men, and I waved. They all lifted their glasses and nodded their heads.

"How about I refresh all you ladies' glasses.

"Yes, you can," said Tasha, and I gave her a look.

"WHAT?! He offered, I'm not turning down no free drinks. That IS a fine brotha, like yourself," she said. He motioned the waiter to bring another round of what we were drinking.

"Maybe we all could do a little adventure together, a trip while we are here?"

"Maybe," I said. "And thank you for the drink."

"My pleasure," he said and walked away. Pamela eyed Sheldon as he walked away.

"He is fine; that's the man you need instead of that no-good Erick."

"Pamela, please don't start. We are here to have a good time."

I raised my glass to toast; our food came, and we ate

laughing, telling jokes, and by the time we noticed the time, the place was getting ready to close.

****

A knock at my complex door; Erick opened it to the same woman who hit him with the bottle back at the club. She entered my home.

"WOW, she must be loaded," she said.

"Yes, she is, and that bitch ass father of hers too."

"So, why not just take her out and leave her parents out of this?" She asked.

"Because her father has my brother's blood on his hands, too, they should have worked a little harder to give my brother the best deal possible. But instead, they failed and caused my only blood relative to get killed in that prison. So, they are all going to pay. If we cover our tracks and do what we planned, nobody will know it was us. You, me, and Kitty are the masterminds of this. We'll rob them dry, fly off to Mexico, and chill on the beach. How do you like that?" Erick said.

"I love it, baby," and she kissed Erick.

He scooped her off her feet, took her to my bedroom, and fucked her on my sheets.

***

I woke up feeling better than I ever did. I tried calling Erick again, and finally, he picked up.

"Hey, baby, I've been calling you."

"Sorry, Boo was taking care of some business. How's your trip."

"Babe, it is gorgeous here. Do you miss me?" I asked.

"Yeah yeah, I miss you, boo. Can't wait for you to come back to me," Erick said.

The woman lying next to Erick woke up, scooted over to him, and began kissing his neck. Then, she started talking, "Who you talking ...." Erick motioned for her to be quiet.

"Erick? Erick! Is someone with you?"

"Naw Naw, I'm out handling some business. In fact, I see the person who I need to see. I gotta go, Melinda."

A slap went across the girl's face. Erick, with rage, shouted "What the fuck! What did I tell you?! When I'm on the phone, shut the fuck up!"

"Baby, I-I- I am sorry," she stuttered.

Then, blow by blow, her cheeks were red, and her lip busted with one last hit from Erick's fist. "Now get over here and suck this dick."

***

I ordered room service for breakfast; fruit, a waffle, scrambled eggs, toast, grits, orange juice, and hazelnut coffee. After breakfast, the girls and I walked to the beach and found a nice spot to sit and enjoy the view of the water. I wore a nice two-piece pink and black trimmed bathing suit while Pamela wore a baby blue and green two-piece suit and Tasha, the skimpiest tight yellow bathing suit with a yellow g- string, covered by a lace skirt. While Sasha wore a whole piece polka-dotted bathing suit that even my mom wouldn't dare to wear at the backyard pool. I understood she is almost a pastor's wife and faithful to her husband.

While we were relaxing in the warm sun, the men at the restaurant came walking our way.

"Hello again, ladies," Sheldon Mitchell said, "It's a pleasure to meet you again. Let me introduce my frat brothers: Jamal Taylor, Frankie Scott, and Travis Freeman," each of them shook our hands and said their hellos. I introduced my girls to them, as well.

I hated to admit they looked Hella sexy with well-built, fresh-cut even goatee, mustache, and low fade cuts except for Jamal Taylor. He had nice locs that fell past his shoulders. I had to hold my composure. I did have a man back at home. The introductions ended with the eight of us agreeing to go on a tour and visit the beautiful land of Costa Rica together. I knew as they departed that the conversations were going to start among my girls.

"DAMN, heaven is missing some fine ass angels, and I'm taking one to my room tonight," shouted Tasha.

"You're not lying. I'm with you on that one," shouted Pamela as they high-fived each other.

"I am a happily married woman," said Sasha, "But my, oh my, they look good."

I laughed. Y'all chill; we are ladies, not sluts."

"Girl, both you and Sasha have men at home; let me and Pamela get some of this action and get laid for a chance," said Tasha.

I let the girls fantasize about which of the four men they wanted to bang their backs out. Then, lotioned myself with my shea butter suntan cream, placed my shades on, and relaxed as I thought about Erick, wondering if he was telling the truth.

***

Later that evening, feeling the fresh warm water on my body as I showered, I couldn't help that I missed Erick's touch as I laid my back on the cool wall of the shower. I lifted up my right leg, placing it on the soap dish, playing with my pussy; I pinched my clit with my fingers. I imagine Erick's lips sucking and kissing my lips while getting a good motion. I placed two fingers inside me. I noticed my shower head could come off the wall as I set the setting to what seemed like a water hose method. I held on to the showerhead and lowered it to my pussy. I let the water tickle my clit, and I moaned, pretending it was Erick's tongue. I held tight to the curtain rod and kept the water at a good angle. My clit vibrated, and my legs began to shake. I climaxed inside the shower, and it felt so amazing. I got out and wrapped myself in a towel, put on my nightgown, and slept like a newborn baby.

58

Chapter Four

Our time was cut short as we agreed to head back home four days early because a storm was headed toward the island. We got our things packed and ready. While waiting near the front lobby, I decided not to call Erick. I wanted to surprise him and show off the sexy outfits I had chosen to wear for him. I hope Erick is ready for me when I get home. I have been horny for his touch since my arrival on the island. I pretended not to see Pamela and Jamal kiss and then exchange phone numbers before they both came walking my way.

Jamal greeted me, "Good morning."

"Hello," I said.

"Sad to see ya'll go; wish we could all do some more sightseeing."

I smiled and took a sip of my hot hazelnut coffee. Tasha and Frankie walked side by side to join the small chit-chat. Sasha arrived by herself. Sheldon and Travis came tagging along afterward, and we said our goodbyes. Sheldon gave me his business card, hoping I would put a word into my father to grant him an interview to work at the law firm.

The plane ride was a success. Pamela and I took a cab together and made it back home safely. We hugged and made plans to speak to each other later. I pressed the elevator door closed. Holding onto my suitcase handle, I was so excited to see Erick.

When I opened the door to my complex, I was greeted by a total mess. What seemed to be my favorite bottle of wine, two were empty, and two of my best crystal glasses were on the table. Not to mention, along with black high-heel pumps, were Erick's pants and shirt. As I went down the hallway, I found a female's gray dress on the floor.

No, this mutha fucker don't have a bitch in my house, I screamed in my mind. But as I got closer to my room, I heard a loud moaning sound from the other side and Erick calling a female named Stacey. The door was cracked open, and I could see Erick fucking the redbone bitch who clocked his ass with the Heineken bottle at the club from the mirror on my ceiling. This son of a bitch! I thought as I busted the door open to my bedroom. Erick got off her, not seeming surprised, came at me, pulled me by my hair, and threw me on the floor.

"Bitch, your parents didn't teach you manners? Don't you know how to knock?" as he punched me.

I didn't come home for Erick to beat me like a punching bag. I looked up at the woman on my bed, scared to even try to help; she pulled the covers up to cover her naked body and sat there while Erick beat my ass. Then, as I screamed for him to get off me, he dragged me into the hallway.

"Bitch, your ass went away, and I was horny, so I got another bitch to take your place."

Erick returned to my room as I lay there crying and in so much pain. He motioned for the girl to get on top and ride his dick. He closed the door behind him. I tried my best, and I got off the floor. I walked to the other bathroom to clean myself up. I stared in the mirror, thinking *...only to be greeted with a bruised face, a bloody nose, and a busted lip.* I couldn't take any more of Erick's abuse! This was the last time. Then, something clicked into my head, something I had forgotten and now remembered. On my twenty-first birthday, my father took me to the gun range to shoot a gun for the first time and gave me a box with pink and gold trimming with a white bow. Inside the box was a black case. I opened it- there lying in the case was a silver 9mm pistol. My mother disagreed with me having a gun, but my father told me later in my life I might need it, and today was the right time to need it.

I went back to my room. Great, this ass hole locked the door. I heard more and more moaning from the other side of the room. I stepped back, closed my eyes, and pulled the trigger. BOOM. I heard a loud scream from the woman. I thought for a moment, *What the fuck Melinda? What did you do?* But that was short-lived as Erick came to the door. Aiming, I had the pistol in his face.

"Baby, be careful with that thing," he said as he raised his hands. I looked over, and the girl Stacey was holding her right breast, screaming. She must have been still riding Erick's dick; the bullet missed Erick's head by a few inches.

I looked back at Erick as I heard him say, "Melinda, give me the gun, baby, please."

"You think I'm stupid, you fucking another bitch in my bed. I gave you a place to stay, and you do this to me. I should kill you right here."

"Baby, I'm sorry, I need help, Boo. We can work this out, come on, forget about her. It's you and me."

I pulled the trigger back as Erick was getting more aggravated and moved to charge at me to take the gun from my hand. Pulling the trigger as my eyes closed, I heard another Boom! I opened my eyes and saw Erick drop to the floor as he screamed in excruciating pain and extreme agony. Cursing through the pain, he managed to speak a sentence.

"Y-ou cr-az-y bi-bitch, y-you sho-shot mee?!

Looking at his hands, I noticed I shot Erick in his dick. "What a good piece of meat," I said.

Erick, withering in pain, managed to grab a towel off the floor while clinging to his penis and holding the area for pressure. I was shocked at what I had just done, but Erick deserved it. He sat breathing heavily, sweat coming from his forehead. If I didn't do anything, both would be dead on my bedroom floor. I grabbed some towels from my bathroom closet and gave Stacey one to add more pressure to the wound. When I got to Erick, his eyes were getting weak.

"Baby, hold on, I'm sorry, I said.

But as I came close to Erick with a towel, he took his left hand and planted it on my throat. I tried to fight him off me while trying to breathe, and my right hand reached for the gun.

Boom, the gun went off again, and Erick's lifeless body was on the floor. I became aware of what I had done, yet still, in shock, I heard myself.

"Erick, wake up, baby, Erick, please, baby, wake up." *Oh my God, what have I done?*

"Baby, I'm so sorry," I said as I sat and watched Erick's lifeless body on my bedroom floor. On my bed, the woman he had was screaming and holding her right breast, putting pressure on the gunshot wound.

I tried to conduct CPR on Erick, but I knew there wasn't any hope. He was dead. I killed my man. I heard the police sirens and an ambulance coming down the road to my complex.

Oh, fuck, who called the police........? I thought.

The police came bursting into my room as I was conducting CPR, and the gun was next to me.

"Freeze," said one of the officers, and "Push the weapon away from you, ma'am."

I pushed the gun to the officer as he kicked it away and cuffed me. Please help him. I didn't mean to shoot him. The officer took me away and let the paramedics do their jobs on Erick and Stacey. Pamela came rushing down the hall to my complex.

"What happened, Melinda?"

"Call my father, please," I blurted out as I was escorted away in cuffs.

***

My face was broadcast on tv and in the newspaper. I didn't deserve to be locked up, especially after what Erick did to me. This was self-defense. I waited for my phone call. Orange is the new black as I glance at myself in a small mirror in the bathroom. My father was back home, doing everything he could to get me out of jail. I called my father with my one phone call he answered on the first ring.

"Daddy, I'm so. "He interrupted me. "Baby girl, it's okay. I will get you out and hire you the best lawyer for your case."

"Daddy, I want Pamela to handle my case. Please, please let Pamela help me. She knows me best."

My father said, okay.

"I love you, daddy, and I'm so sorry."

"Love you too."

I cried myself to sleep.

***

Leaving to get into the police car to head to court. Camera crews were everywhere. I tried to cover my face with my hands as their lights flashed left and right.

***

All raised for the honorable Judge Janet King. I knew Judge King; I was often in her courtroom with cases. I looked behind my shoulder; on the front row were my father and mother. Tasha and Sasha were spotted in the back where everybody from the law firm sat, including Donna. On the other side of the room, I spotted none other than Johnathon Cane's shady ass.

"Ms. Melinda Stone, what a surprise to see you in my courtroom in a time and matter like this."

I lowered my head in shame. I couldn't say anything. Once the jury came and took their seats, the court session started. Arguments, objections, and disagreements were coming from left to right, and I stared at the jury. They were like statues glued to each and every detail. I was so afraid that I would get the maximum sentence, which was life in prison without parole. Finally, tired of the bickering, Judge King announced that the court would go into recess for two days and resume at 8 am. I waved goodbye to my family and friends and followed the officer to head back to my new home. I couldn't sleep that night; I was having nightmares about Erick. It felt so real I couldn't believe Erick was gone. Deep down, I still loved Erick.

Late last night, Pamela was awakened by a phone call. She didn't recognize the number nor the voice on the other line. "I want to testify for Melinda. I want to help her. Please put me on the witness stand."

"Who is this?" Pamela asked.

"I'm Stacey Washington, the woman that Melinda accidentally shot."

Pamela paused for a moment. "Okay, could you meet me at my office tomorrow around 1 pm so I can get your statement?" She agreed and hung up the phone. The following day Stacey came to see Pamela. Pamela was shocked about all the info that Stacey told her. Okay, this is useful information Pamela jotted down the address on when and what time to be at court. Stacey walked away, and Pamela rushed to see me in jail.

"We may win this case!" said Pamela.

She filled me in on what just happened at her office. She was alive! That yellow bitch who was fucking my man in my bed was alive. So much relief came from my chest. Pamela continued with her update.

"Her name is Stacey Washington, and she may be the golden ticket to help you."

"How is she?"

"She's doing good, she managed to survive with a few surgeries, and the doctor had to take out her right breast implant. Once she heals, she can probably try and do another breast operation."

"I'm glad she's okay," I said.

"Well, I'll see you tomorrow in court," Pamela said and got up and left.

At lunch, I sat next to the television and saw on the news a lady who committed suicide in her own home with an apology letter to her family; her name was unknown. Early that morning, before court, my father brought a nice suit for me to wear. As I prepared for court, my face slightly bruised, I cried as I envisioned Erick beating me. If he could, he would have left me dead from his beatings. I rode in the back of the cop car and was on my way to court. Everyone showed up again for court, and of course, Johnathon Cane was sitting in the same spot, grinning like the cat from Alice in Wonderland.

"All rise, court's now in session, the honorable Judge Janet King presiding."

As the jury took their seats, the court began where we left off. Stacey Washington came in extremely late, and by the looks of it, she looked like she hadn't gotten any sleep. Her eyes were puffy like she had been crying all night.

"Sorry, I'm late," she said as she took her seat and waited to be called to the witness stand. Back and forth, Pamela was doing a fabulous job getting her point across and winning the jury's attention as David Williams was dragging me into the mud, stating I must have planned to kill Erick Tyson eventually. Finally, I had enough of his beatings, enough of his lies.

"Does the defense have any witnesses?" said Judge King. "Yes, your honor, I would like to call Stacey Washington to the stand," said Pamela.

Stacey came in looking so pale and weak that the judge had to ask if she was okay. She agreed she was fine. As Pamela went toward Stacey to tell her side of the story. My heart dropped. She looked directly at me and spoke.

"Melinda, I'm so sorry, but Erick knew you from the start."

"WHAT?!" I said as I jumped up from my seat.

"Sit down, Ms. Stone," yelled the judge.

"Go on," said the judge.

"He knew you all along. He wanted revenge; he wanted to kill you and your family for the murder of his brother Rico Jackson aka Silk."

I wanted to die right there, I graduated from my classes in college early, and my father decided I should take my first case. I got the case of Rico Jackson, aka Silk, one of the biggest drug dealers. He transferred drugs to different cities and states and made a fortune. Silk thought he could trust his right-hand man, Sammie Watson, but little did Silk know Sammie was trying to go solo and take half of Silk's products, half his customers, and go off on his own. When Silk confronted him and how he was missing over three pounds of a kilo. Silk was heated, and as they went to their hideout under an abandoned bridge, Silk didn't know there was a witness. While taking a stroll, a woman named Kelly Bush saw Silk kill Sammie in cold blood. I did everything I could but lost the trial. Silk was given the maximum sentence, life in prison with no parole. After two months in prison, Silk was killed. Little did he know Sammie was a bit popular inside. He helped smuggle drugs for his older brother Justin Watson aka Cash. When Cash and some of his gang member friends heard the news that Sammie was dead and that Silk was the one who killed him, they plotted to take him out. Silk was stabbed six times in the stomach and rushed to the hospital, but he died from his injuries.

Stacey, who was still on the witness stand, sobbed continuously. "I'm sorry for my emotional behavior," she said.

As she was still telling how Erick blamed me for his brother's death. I jotted on a piece of paper and scribbled a note for Pamela. Pamela looked at the paper and asked, "You sure?" I nodded.

Pamela asked her a question. "Ms. Washington, did you know the deceased Kitty?"

"Yes, she and I were good friends working for Erick to take revenge on Melinda and her family."

I couldn't believe it; as Stacey explained, Kitty was her nickname, and Kitty was Silk's leading lady. They discuss marriage and starting a family once Silk built his drug empire. Her real name is Victoria Peterson.

"It can't be," I murmured as my mother yelled from behind me. Was she related to Otis Peterson?

"Order in the court. Ms. Stone, please sit down, or I will have you escorted out."

"Be quiet and sit down, Martha." My father tugged on my mother's arm.

"Yes, ma'am, that was her father, and she was your sister Melinda."

" WHAT THE FUCK?" I blurted out.

"Order! Order in the court! That goes for you too," shouted Judge King.

Otis Peterson is a high-paid architect. As I thought to myself, *my birth father is loaded. Maxwell will always and forever will be my father. Fuck Otis.*

When Mr. Peterson discovered that his daughter was dating a drug dealer, he tried to move her to his parents, but Victoria still had contact with Silk. He gave her an ultimatum to either come home and focus on getting on the right path or be with Silk. She chose Silk. Mr. Peterson took everything from her, canceled her credit cards, and removed her from his Will.

"Damn, that's cold," I said to myself.

Even though I did a terrible thing, my father still has me covered. I couldn't believe all that Stacey said on the witness stand. I honestly thought Erick loved me. Stacey talked about how she and Erick grew up together as kids, dropped out of high school, and ran off together. With all the abuse Erick was doing to her, she had three miscarriages. My heart broke as I watched her sobbing.

"Okay, let's take an hour lunch break," said Judge King.

Before getting taken to the back, I jotted on another piece of paper and passed it to Pamela. The note said,

"Let Stacey get probation. I will take what's given to me; she's been through enough."

Lunch was over, and the court was back in session. Pamela was confused about my suggestion, and I wouldn't change my mind. I repeatedly told her, don't fight with me. Just do it.

"Are we ready to continue, Ms. Tucker, Ms. Tucker, are we ready to continue?" said Judge King.

"I'm sorry, your honor; we are ready."

Too upset with my choice and decision. Pamela stood up and called me to the stand. I told everything about how I met Erick and that I didn't know anything about his plan to kill my family or me. Then, I looked up and saw tears in my father's eyes. I should have told him, but I thought I could handle the situation on my own. The jurors remained still, listening to everything.

"I just hope you all have a heart and know I didn't mean for all this to happen," were my final words on the stand.

The jury deliberation was taking extremely long. I watched the clock on the wall, tick-tock in the small cube of a room as I waited to go back to court to hear the jury's verdict.
Pamela did so well. I was so proud of how she handled my case. My hands were sweaty, and I wasn't feeling well, sick to my stomach. Nervous that I may not see my family and friends again.

Back in the courtroom

"Has the jury reached a verdict?" asked Judge King.

"Yes, your honor, we've found Melinda Stone GUILTY."

NNNNOOOOOO, as everyone on my side screamed. I cried in the palm of my hands like a baby. I held my hand forward for the officer to place the cuffs on. For the first time, I saw my mother with tears in her eyes.

"I will be praying for you, girl," Sasha said as I waved my goodbyes and exited out the door. Pamela came to visit me and notified me of a plea deal.

"I got the best deal for you. Your father and I pulled some strings; take this deal, Melinda."

I took the piece of paper and read over everything.
"I don't belong here Pamela, and did you help Stacey?"

"Yes, I did; she got three years of probation."

"Great," I responded as I took the pen out of Pamela's hand and signed my signature.

For the next five years, I would be in a hell hole called prison.

PART TWO
Repercussions

Chapter Five

Months later

No, don't hurt me. Don't take my baby. Please, take me instead. My hands were tied to a pipe as I stood up, begging for the man in a black mask to let go of my son. I was surrounded by old barrels and the smell of rust. The man approached me and caressed my cheek. I tried to snatch it away.

"If it's money you need, I can provide for you. My father is Maxwell Stone. Whatever amount of money you need, he will give it to you. Please don't hurt my baby."

The strange man shouted I don't want no fucking money bitch, not just yet anyway. What I want, I already got right here as he held onto Erickson.

"Please, please," I said, "My son is all I got."

"Melinda, Melinda, wake up, girl."

I opened my eyes to see my cellmate Judith Greene, aka Money, who got the nickname Money by robbing a few banks. She shot a teller and the security guard.

"Having that same nightmare again," Money said. "I swear, girl, you need to talk to someone about what's happening. You been talking and screaming in your sleep since you got here."

"Sorry, maybe you're right. I need to talk to someone." I got up from my bunk, and I felt a sharp pain in my stomach. My water broke.

On February 19, at 9:05 pm, I gave birth to my beautiful son Erickson Maxwell Stone, a split image of his father. I named him after my two favorite men who I loved. Not a day goes by that I don't think about Erick. I wish he could have had the chance to meet his son, let alone know that I was pregnant. My parents decided to take care of my baby until I was released from prison and promised they would bring him to every visit for me to see him. Seeing my father wrap my baby in a blue blanket with his initials sewed in the middle, I thought, I don't want to become like my mother. I wanted my son to be there for him, but being stuck in prison, I can't be the mother I could be to him.

"He will be well taken care of, baby girl. I'll make sure he has everything he needs," said my father. My father retired soon after my court case, and he made Pamela the new boss of his firm. I knew my father's firm was in good hands. She was a better lawyer and took it more seriously than I did. I missed spending time with my girl; Tasha and Frankie were a couple, and Pamela and Jamal were off and on. Apparently, Jamal's ex-fiancé was having a hard time and couldn't let him go.

"How are you feeling?" Money asked.

Money had my back since I transferred to the women's state prison. She didn't let any of the other women bother me whatsoever, with all I had to deal with alone, my depression and pregnancy.

Money was there for me; she wasn't Erick, but she did fill my needs. Her touch took me to a place in my college years. Pamela and I were roommates until graduation. One night we got so wasted, and well, one thing led to another. Pammie's touch was so warm, so smooth. Her lips kissing my nude breast felt like a delicate flower. She kissed my belly button, and her tongue made a wet trail down to my pussy.

Even though this was our first time, and we didn't know what we were doing, we were so intimate with one another that what we were doing felt so right. All through college until graduation, Pamela and I never seemed to be a part, so we decided to get a place on our own. Living in the same complex, I gave Pammie a key, and any time she wanted me, she was welcomed to my home, and we made passionate love to each other. Pamela and I made a pact that we would never tell the girls, and now that we are adults, we still held on to that pact.

It's been a while since Pamela and I slept together. She rarely used my key until I met and got serious with Erick. I wonder if it was a rage of jealousy that Pammie had over Erick.

Money was like both Erick and Pamela. Hardcore protective like Erick and sweet, kind, and caring like Pamela. Money took me back to that night but so much better than what Pamela and I were doing. Money was a professional as she took her time with me, not because I was pregnant.

Her tongue was sucking gently on my clit as I moaned softly in my pillow. Money promised me once I gave birth, she'd give me something I never had before.

****

"Wat a gwaan," said Spice. Spice was similar to Tasha, ratchet with street talk. Her Jamaican platform body, buttery brown skin, and accent let everyone know in the facility that she was there.

"So let me get this straight, you gwaan and shot cha dude and is pregnant with his baby."

Half of the time, nobody barely knew what Spice was saying, but she was an outspoken woman. Spice was sentenced to fifteen years. She poisoned her stepfather, who sexually assaulted her since she was nine years old. The crazy thing is that her mother knew about the rape but never told anyone. Her mother didn't want to testify on behalf of her daughter.

"Leave her alone," said Kee-Kee.

Kee- Kee, she a badass bitch. This crazy bitch caught her husband with her sister and ended up hiring two thugs to burn her house while they were in it. The plan almost worked. They all covered their tracks, and she almost got away with murder. She had a huge chunk of her husband's insurance money until one of the thugs opened up his big mouth and told what had happened.

Little did he know he was talking to an undercover cop who was wired, so he had to snitch and tell who was all involved. As a result, Kee-Kee is on death row, and the two thugs are serving life in prison.

"I'm not letting Spice get under my skin Kee-Kee, so you good girl," I said.

"Well, well, well, I see someone a little bit different. You not pregnant no more, so, talk all that shit now and get your ass beat bitch," yelled Cleo. I backed my chair back from the table and was in Cleo's face.

"Don't fucking start with me, Cleo."

I pushed her with both hands on her shoulder. Cleo almost slapped me until Money grabbed her hand and punched her in the gut. Fight! Fight, fight, all the ladies in the cafeteria shouted out loudly. Officer Kim Hodge and her crew came rushing to us while we went in on Cleo and her crew.

"Break it up, ladies, right now!" Officer Hodge shouted.

"I'm sick of her shit," I scream out.

"Ms. Stone, you need to show a little more class and respect. For God's sake, you are the best lawyer's daughter, and you are acting like this. What will Mr. Maxwell say if he hears about this? You don't want to serve extra time in here. Your baby boy needs you."

You're right, Officer Hodge, I thought inwardly, keeping it to myself and fixing myself up. I headed back to my cell. I wiped the blood that came from Cleo's lips with a napkin.

Later that night, all I could think about was my little bundle of joy. My father said he would mail me a picture of him when he writes me, and I knew I would tape them to my wall. As I cried softly, not trying to wake up Money. I heard Money ease off from the top bunk and sit next to me.

"What's wrong, Melinda?"

I sat there sobbing, telling her how I felt. She gently wiped my tears with her fingertips and pulled me close to her. Money's a thick BBW chick; her breast cup size was 40DDD. She gently kissed my forehead. I lifted my face, and my lips locked to hers. We kissed so passionately as our tongues danced in each other's mouths. She slid her hands down my orange pants, and her fingertips gently made their way to my wet pussy.

I lay down while spreading my legs. Money slid off my pants along with my wet cotton underwear and took me to paradise. She sucked on my clit like I was fucking vanilla ice cream on a cone. My juices and Money's salvia trickled down my thighs as I ground my hips closer and closer to her lips. My eyes rolled to the back of my head as I tried to hold my moans. Money raised her head and asked if I was ready for what she promised me after I had Erickson. I nodded yes. She grabbed my hands and stood me up from the bed. She placed my bare-naked ass on the cold bars. Then, taking two of her scarves, she tied my hands, raised my legs off the floor, and ate my pussy like it was no fucking tomorrow. As she raised my ass up and down on her tongue, I tilted my head to the side. Money had me climax till I lost count. I opened my eyes straight ahead. I saw Spice's crazy-ass smiling from ear to ear in the darkness like she wished she was right in our cell, joining the fun. Spice was sitting up, and what appeared like she was fingering herself as I saw her cover move while she raised her left leg. I enjoyed every moment of Money last night. I woke up to the sound of the officers screaming for everyone to get up.

Money greeted me with a kiss and asked me how she did last night. I kissed her back and said I enjoy every piece of you. In my mind, I wished that once I got out, Money could come with me. But I knew that couldn't happen, and I didn't want the girls to know what the fuck I was doing in prison. I didn't want to tell them the facts: *when I'm horny, I let my cellmate eat my pussy until I climax every other night.* I damn sure can't let Pammie know. We both agreed to not be with another woman. After being here, I forgot about the contract Pamela, and I created and signed a long time ago. When I get back home, I have to burn the contract we signed and agreed on. Hell, after being grown with our own life, I figured that the contract wasn't real anyway; we were college kids.

***

I got a surprise today, a visit from my father and son. He was getting so big. I played and cooed with him, kissed his little hands, and held him as the tears ran down my face. My father had to inform me everything would be okay and that my son was in good hands. He tells him about me every day and lets Erickson know that I love him so much.

"Listen, baby girl, five years may seem long, but it will end quickly, in a blink of an eye."

I smiled and continued playing with Erickson. My father informed me that the firm was doing very well with Pamela. She moved into my office, and Sasha and Tasha come by and help with Erickson every day.

"It is so good to have a baby around the house. I'm retired, and my grandson keeps me busy," said my father.

Visiting time was almost over. I placed Erickson back into my father's arms, kissed my baby gently on the forehead, kissed my father on his cheek, and watched them leave past the glass doors. I went back to my cell and lay there till I fell asleep. Days, weeks, months, and years flew by as I saw my baby boy grow up. Finally, the fifth year came, and I was too excited to leave this hell hole. I know I won't be returning here as I waited for the final day to come for my release.

"Don't forget about your girl," said Money as I smiled and hugged her. I told her how I appreciated her having my back and being there for me. She kissed me so gently, and that night, Money and I made love. Since being Money's cellmate, I wanted to know how her body tasted.

As I caressed and sucked Money's huge breast in my mouth, she tried to hold back her moans. But couldn't control her urge much longer. I gently made my way to Money's wet pussy, and in a circular motion, I played with her clit as her juices ran between my fingers. I finally released her clit and sucked my fingers to taste her sweet nectar. Money has done so much for me and my sexual desires. It was time that I returned the favor; I got on my knees and had Money spread her legs. My tongue tasted and entered her wet walls.

Money's juices were dripping down my chin. Without making a lot of noise, I sucked on her pussy lips as she tried her best not to moan loud; and cause a scene waking up the other inmates or have the guards come to find out what was all the noise happening at three o'clock in the morning. Money was on the verge of climax but stopped me as she lifted my face and sucked her juices off my tongue. She picked me up onto her top bunk and returned the favor; as her warm tongue entered my pussy. I realized after tonight this would be my last night with her.

I sat anxiously waiting for the court to order my release and the five-year sentence to end to go home to my family. Finally, Judge Janet King granted my release, and I was free to go. As I got my belongings and was headed to leave, giving my girls hugs and saying goodbye, don't gwana back, take care of yourself, gurl said Spice.

I couldn't find where Money was. I wanted to see her and let her know I would transfer all my money from my books to hers. As I walked farther down the hall, I stopped Kee-Kee, and she told me that Money had gotten herself into the hole.

Cleo constantly kept fucking with my girl, and she got her ass dealt with. I tried to find a way to see Money, and luckily, I had my chance with Ms. Hodge.

"You know I could get in serious trouble'" she said.

"Yeah, I know, but I just want to say my final goodbye to her."

I walked through the doors, and Money was lying in the bunk at the end.

Her face was so bruised. "Money, I'm leaving, and I want to thank you for all you have done for me. I don't know what I would have done without you."

Money got up, came to me, and caressed my cheeks, wiping the tears from my face.

"I'm going to fucking miss you, Melinda, " Money said.

I kissed her lips one last time. We got so passionate in our kiss that I didn't realize my name was being called from the loudspeaker, "Melinda Stone..."

I didn't want to say goodbye to Money. But she forced me to leave.

"Go girl, go home to your son and family."

My baby boy, I missed five years already. I miss so much of his life. As I walked off, I heard Money say, "Melinda, I love you." I ran back to her and replied that I loved her too.

Chapter Six

The doors closed behind me with a final buzz. I was finally free after five years of being inside a women's prison. The warm sun hit my face, and the cool breeze blew through my hair. But, God, I needed something done to my hair. My curls had gotten so dry and brittle. I knew I had to hit somebody's shop to get a fresh new makeover. As I glanced around the parking lot, I spotted my son standing next to my father, Maxwell. Pamela, Tasha, and Sasha were standing by the car waving me down. I ran to greet them, so happy to be free and out. We all cried in each other's arms.

"We missed you bitch!" shouted Tasha's ghetto ass. "I missed ya'll too."

The tears kept coming hard and heavy.

"DADDY!" I shouted as I hugged him tight and kissed him on his cheeks.

Smiling, he couldn't continue to contain his inner joy; while embracing me, he stated, "My baby girl is finally coming home."

I leaned over and saw Erickson holding on to my father's pants leg.

"Erickson, this is mommy. Remember all the pictures in your baby book of mommy and you."

Erickson nodded his little head, walked over to me, and smiled. His two front teeth were missing, "Hello, I'm Erickson, and I'm five years old." He placed his little hands up, showing me five. Looking at his little hand, I asked…" Can I have a hug?"

"Yes, mommy, you can have a hug and a big kiss," he said as he jumped into my arms. I couldn't let him go. His warm hug and kisses filled my heart.

"Where's mommy," I said to my father.

"Your mother couldn't make it. She is at home waiting to see you there."

We got into my father's SUV; Tasha wanted all the details of what I had been doing for the past five years while locked up. I told her we would talk about that later. But, first, I wanted to get the 411 with Pamela as she bragged about having my old office and Donna as her assistant. I was interested in how much she did for the firm, with new clients and winning so many cases. I couldn't be prouder of her. Sasha had to put her two cents in before we arrived at my parent's house.

"Well, Melinda, I want you to give your life to Christ. So, I want to invite you to my church this coming Sunday, where my man preaches a good message," said Sasha.

Considering my thoughts in prison, "Of course, Sasha, I will love to come."

We arrived at my parent's house. After five straight years, my mother was still the same person. "Look at yourself, Melinda; you look a mess. You gained weight, and your hair," shaking her head as she looked me up and down.

"Hello, mother," I said. "How have you been?"

"Ladies, ladies, please, this is a celebration. Finally, our baby girl is home; Martha, at least you should have some type of joy in your heart that she is finally home," said my father. Sucking her teeth, my mother replies, "Let's eat dinner before the food gets cold."

Sasha blessed the food, and we all sat in silence eating. *Damn, eating with the girls in prison was better than this bullshit.* I thought to myself.

After dinner, the girls departed, and I ran Erickson a bath and put him to bed. He had my brother Devin's old room decoration of hot wheels cars filled the room. Across from his bed was a picture of baby Erickson and me. My father took the picture after giving birth to my son in the hospital. I leaned over Erickson as he slept in the bed. Kissing him on his cheek, I whispered into his ear and said, "Mommy will never leave you again."

My old room was across the hall, and the décor was still the same. Nothing was removed or touched. My queen-sized bed was neatly made with pink and gold silk sheets. Trophies I had won from childhood to my teenage years filled the shelves. I walked into my bathroom and ran a hot bath. As I soaked, all I could think about was Money.

How bad I needed her touch to ease away the stress I was having right now. I really needed somebody, and since it couldn't be Money. I might as well call Pammie. I reached for my phone off the tub's platform and called her. Pamela answered after just one ring.

"Can you come over?" I said before she could say hello.

"I need you like old times since Erick is..."

Pamela interrupted, "I'll be right over, unlock the door."

I felt like a kid again, sneaking over to a friend's house only to come inside while the parents were sleeping. Pamela came, and instantly we rushed back to my old room, and she gave me more than what I expected. I was in for a surprise. Pamela pulls out a strap that she slips on, and in the hole, she slips on a rubber 10-inch Carmel dick.

"Are you ready?" Pamela asked in the moonlit, dimmed room. I lustfully nodded yes. Pamela kissed my perky nipples and sucked gently on them like they were gumdrops. As I moaned softly in her ear, I kissed her collarbone then she planted wet kisses down my belly button as she pinched my clit with her fingertips. I jumped from the excitement. Pamela was between my legs like old times, eating my pussy. The feeling of her tongue and the way it vibrated on my clit made me recall what we did back in college.

I massaged her bob-length hair in my hands, and the thought of Money came to my mind; a flashback of Money and I in the cell each night and the pleasure of her touch that made me climax. I almost shouted

Money's name out loud when Pamela raised her head, quickly sliding up my body, looking directly into my face, her hand directed and inserted the strap-on dick inside my throbbing pussy. I didn't want her to stop as I felt each stroke Pamela did to my pussy. I was so tight, and I needed it. Erick was the only dick I had since going to prison. At this point, I didn't care; I was being fucked so good by a fake one. Pamela was taking care of me, right. As I wrapped my legs around her waist, she drilled the dick deeper inside my walls. I wanted to scream loud but had to control myself, not wake up Erickson or my parents. As sweat dripped from Pamela's forehead to my lips, I licked her sweat off my lips and gently dug my fingernails into her back.

Once finished, Pamela got off me and laid down on my pillow as the strap dick was still on her with all my juices. I unhooked and took off the strap-on and went to work. As I sucked and placed two fingers inside Pamela's pussy, she grinded her hips rhythmically on my tongue. Her moans were becoming loud as I had to remind her where we were. Pamela still tasted so sweet. I enjoyed my continued field play on her pussy. Reaching her peak of arousal, she climaxed on my tongue and fingers. I laid there for a moment, too tired to do anything else. Eventually, I placed my head on Pamela's breast as she caressed my thick curly hair in her hands.

"Melinda."

"Yes," I responded.

"Did you mess with anybody while being locked up for those five years?"

I was surprised as to why she asked me this question.

"Pammie, you do realize I was in a female prison, not a male prison?"

She chuckled, "I know that, but I'm curious to know what you've been doing and how you dealt with your sexual desire when you were horny, especially being pregnant with Erickson. I don't have kids, but a pregnant woman's hormones go through the roof, so I heard."

The sound of Pamela's voice felt real, and she was seriously expecting me to answer the question truthfully. But I couldn't, so I had to lie to her. She couldn't see that I was untruthful because it was dark.

"Nobody Pamela. I didn't do anything with anybody. I was making sure I stayed alive, had a healthy baby boy, and focused on coming home to my family. Being away from my son for five years, I can't get that back. At times I felt like I was a bad mother and becoming my own mother. I missed you, Tasha, and even Sasha's holier-than-thou ass. I missed how we hung out, doing what we normally do best together. I felt that once I got out of prison, neither of you girls would want anything to do with me anymore."

I felt Pamela's breast rise and fall as she took a breath to dismiss my thoughts.

"Melinda, you will forever be my best friend, my sister; we shared so much history together. Look at what we are doing now. I cherish this secret forever, and I promise nobody will find out about us. I love you, girl. It devastated me how Erick treated you. Honestly, at that point in time, I wanted to see if we could take us to the next level. But you had your ass in Erick's behind and so much in love with him that I couldn't tell you how I felt. My feelings for you are the same as they were with you back in college; my feelings for you are still strong."

Pamela held me so tight that night. We slept soundly in each other's arms. I woke up to Erickson shaking me while rubbing his eyes.

"Mommy, I'm hungry."

I jumped up, and so did Pamela. I told Erickson to hurry back to his room, and we would go downstairs for me to prepare him some cereal.

"Dammit, I thought you locked the door," I shouted to Pamela.

"NO, I thought you did," said Pamela.

"Besides, he's a kid; he doesn't know what we did."

She planted a kiss on my shoulder. I got dressed and ran to Erickson's room, put on his slippers, and we went downstairs to prepare breakfast. Great, there wasn't any hazelnut coffee insight, so I brewed up some black coffee and sat next to Erickson, watching my son eat his cereal.

"Slow down, son. I don't want you to choke; chew your food, right," I said as he smiled while still taking a spoonful of cereal in his tiny mouth.

****

I heard him before I saw him.

"Good morning," I said as he placed a kiss on my head.

My father smiling, looked at me with a questioning look.

"Morning to you. How did you sleep back in your old room? I never thought you'd be back here again," he chuckled.

"I slept great, daddy, and it feels so good to be back home."

"That's wonderful, Melinda," he paused, looking concerned. "I was thinking, what are you going to do about your condo? Have you made any plans to move back or put it on the market for sale?"

Before I could answer, Pamela walked toward us.

"She should sell it. It has too many bad memories to go back to," she said.

"Pamela," my father shouted. "I didn't know you were here."

"Good morning, Mr. Maxwell. Yeah, I came over late last night, and Melinda and I had a few drinks; it was late, and I didn't want to drive home drunk."

"You know you are always welcome here; you are like a daughter to me," said my father while my mother went to prepare breakfast. We sat in silence afterward.

***

I got Erickson ready for school, and for the first time, I entered his school and walked my little boy to his class.

"See you later, mommy," shouted Erickson as he gave me a hug and kiss. I walked back to Pamela's car, and we headed to my condo to work out the contract to sell my home. Everything was gone. My father placed all my belongings in a storage rental. As I approached my room, the sight of going in scared me. I could still hear the arguments between Erick and me. The walls were freshly painted by my father, and new carpet was on the floors.

"Are you okay?" said Pamela as she caressed my shoulders and kissed me softly on my neck.

"I'm fine," I said. "Have you heard where Stacey is? I want to apologize to her for everything that has happened."

"The last time I heard from her, she was getting help at a local group," Pamela said.

As we were about to exit the building, Thomas, the front deskman, stopped me.

"Excuse me, Ms. Stone, we have some mail for you, and he placed a big bag of unread letters on the counter. *Damn, this is a lot of mail,* I thought.

"Thank you, Thomas," was all I said as I grabbed the mailbag and walked to Pamela's car. Most of the letters were from bill collectors and coupons, but I was surprised to see a few letters from a familiar name. Unaware, I was speaking out loud, "How did he even get my address? How did he know where I lived?"

"Who?" said Pamela.

Showing Pamela, I held six letters in my hand with the name Otis Peterson printed boldly on the envelopes.

Pamela looked at the name and blurted out, "Your father?"

"He IS NOT my father! Maxwell is...remember that, Pamela!"

Placing her hands up to surrender calmed me. "You know what I meant, Melinda."

After a moment of silence, Pamela started the vehicle, looked at the traffic, and pulled out of the complex parking lot; then asked, "Are you going to open the letters?"

*****

I placed each letter in order by the date stamped on my nightstand and walked away.

I sat looking at my son during dinner, and I decided once I put Erickson to bed, I would read what he had to say. *Since the daughter he raised is dead, what does he want with me?* I thought.

Dear Melinda,

As you are reading this, I know you may be wondering why I am contacting you after all this time. I'm genuinely sorry for denying you as my daughter. I knew I was wrong for cheating on my sick wife, she didn't deserve the mistake I caused not saying you were a mistake, but I should have taken care of my responsibility as a man and treated you like my other children. You could have gotten to know your siblings, and I pray that you forgive me one day.

I know you saw on the news about my daughter Victoria Peterson whom people on the streets called Kitty. The story stated that she killed herself. But as a father, I don't think my little girl had the heart to take her own life. Then I read in the papers about your situation where you got five years in prison for killing Erick Tyson. I remember him and his brother. I believe his name was Silk. Both brothers always came to my home to pick up Victoria and caused so much of a scene in the neighborhood. I still don't know what Victoria saw in Silk.

Let me get to the point of why I'm writing to you. I need your help. I know this may sound crazy, but I really need your help. I hired a private investigator on Erick Tyson. I did my research. You need to know that the private investigator and I discovered that Erick's body is missing.

There's no record of a death certificate, burial, or cremation. It is like his body is in the wind. You have a son with him. I hope I can say I'm a grandfather, my first grandson. Also, when you get to this letter, I pray that you find it in your heart to forgive me and find out where the hell Erick is because I believe Victoria was murdered...

P.S. Here is my card; call me when you have the time.
Sincerely,
Otis Peterson

My heart stopped; I was speechless. Erick is alive. NO! I served five years, conducted CPR, and tried to save Erick; he's dead. This can't be right.

Confused, my door opened wide, and my mother rushed into my room. Melinda, you didn't hear Erickson or me calling you? Your son is asking for you... he needs to be bathed and ready for bed, and you up here doing what. She glanced at my bed and saw the envelopes of Otis Peterson.

"What the hell does he want with you," she asked as she snatched the letters off my bed. "It's too late to try and be a father; I'll get rid of these right now."

"Mommy give me my letters, please!" I snatch them out of her hands. I looked at her in disbelief as she stared at me accusingly.

"So, you're going to make amends with this man who destroyed you when you were a child. You're a bigger fool than I thought."

Before walking out, my mother turned around with pain and determination to condemn. She cursed me. "You disobedient bitch!"

I couldn't let the pain of my mother's words hurt me. I had to talk to someone about this. But I had to attend to Erickson first. Somehow the letters called to me after dinner, overriding my plans to have Erickson ready for bed to avoid Mother. I sighed, and as I walked out of the room, I heard my son call my name, "Mommy..."

****

Early Sunday arrived, and Sasha never forgot my promise about coming to Sunday service with her. So, I got myself and Erickson ready and headed to Second Chance Baptist Church. The service was amazing. Sasha's husband, Nick preached a wonderful sermon; I decided to stay after church and help serve the homeless a meal; as I glanced around the room and saw so many homeless people who suffered just trying to find a decent place to stay and a hot meal to eat; I thought I am truly blessed. Unfortunately, my mother has her faults. She could have given me up or abandoned me, but she didn't.

"Melinda, Melinda, are you okay?"

Sasha's voice nudged me from my thoughts, and a man was waiting on me to serve his plate with a roll and vegetables. I noticed the trash was getting full. I told Sasha I was taking out the trash; she pointed toward the trash compactor located in the back. Erickson, seeing me heading outside, wanted to tag along. After dumping the trash, I heard a familiar voice in the little crowd of people hanging outside the church. Before I could even speak her name, she instantly shouted out mine.

"Melinda, is that you? OMG, you're out of prison, girl! You look good. Give me a hug."

We embraced one another as I asked, "Stacey Washington, how have you been?"

"I really want to thank you for allowing your friend to give me probation," she said, -I am so sorry for what you have been through and what I put you through."

"No, No, Stacey, I should be the one apologizing for shooting you, sorry for…. "She didn't let me finish.

"Don't be sorry; it's all good, Melinda, and besides, I'm happy now I'm off drugs. I got clean, and I got married." She shook her hand out and exposed a 1ct. Princess solitaire diamond ring.

"Wow, it's beautiful, congratulations."

"Thank you, Melinda. I got my life turned around and received help from a therapist named Dr. Bradley Lewis," she pulled out his card. "He really is excellent; you should make an appointment with him. He may be of help to you get through everything."

"Thanks, I will give him a call," taking the card from Stacey.

"Mommy, I'm tired," cried Erickson.

Stacey bent down and locked eyes with Erickson while asking, "And who is this little cutie pie."

"This is my son Erickson."

Stacey never looked away from Erickson. "He is so handsome, and he looks just like Erick."

She straightened up with a slight smile on her face, then looking at her phone, she sighed and said, "I should be going."

"Well, it's getting late, Stacey. Take care."

You too, Melinda, she said as she walked away. Erikson and I went back into the building, only to have Sasha look at me like, what took you so long, and where you been.

Stacey's phone rang when she reached her vehicle. A man's voice was on the other end.

"Where the hell are you? You been gone too damn long bitch."

"Babe, I'm coming home now. I ran into an old friend; well, let's say your old friend."

"Who the fuck, you talking about?" Stacey chuckled as he grew impatient with her small talk, no information. "I said Who and What the fuck, you talking about bitch?"

"She was pregnant when she got convicted, served five years, and now has a five-year-old son named Erickson." The phone went silent for a moment, only to hear. "Damn, I'm a father?"

Annoyed by his extended silence, Stacey said, "That could have been my son. I can't believe you got that bitch pregnant. I should be the one and the only woman having your baby."

Speechless, Erick sighed on the phone as he took a deep breath and replied.

"Stacey, you are my wife; now we will deal with having a family soon, but you know what I still want to do. I can't rest until I have all their asses dead. We got our new identities today; Drew dropped them off a few hours ago. I bet that Melinda and her fuck up family think I'm dead, but baby, this time, the table is going to be turned. Let's set this plan in motion, fly somewhere far, and enjoy our happiness together. Bring your ass home." Erick said.

"If this gets out that you aren't dead, we could go to prison for a very long time. I still have nightmares about what we did to…" Erick stopped Stacey in her tracks.

"Listen, nobody wants to find out 'bout anything. You've been riding with me this long. Let's keep on riding together. The call ended just as Stacey looked out of her car's passenger window and saw Melinda drive off and vanish around the corner. Stacey muttered to herself, *"he was supposed to be my son. I will take what's mine BITCH!"*

***

Today had been checked, and I was ready to go to bed, but Pamela and Tasha wanted to grab a couple of drinks. My father insisted that he would watch Erickson, so I could go out and have a good time, hang with my girls, and start having a normal life again. Unfortunately, Sasha couldn't make it. She went with her husband, who had to attend a late luncheon with a few board members about opening a community center to help people in need. So tonight, Pamela, Tasha, and I celebrated my freedom as a free woman. We danced our asses on the dance floor, drinking bottle after bottle of wine. I didn't want the night to end.

All of a sudden, the DJ played Joe- *I wanna know*. I lost my cool, felt uncomfortable, and my vibe dropped from one hundred to zero really quickly.

"Are you alright?" Pamela asked as she stared deeply into my eyes, waiting for a response.

"I'm okay," and I looked at the time; it was almost midnight.

"I better get going; I don't want to stay out too long; I gotta get Erickson ready for school tomorrow."

We hugged each other goodnight. I walked through the dark alley to locate my car. I felt like somebody was following me as the hairs on the back of my neck stood straight up; as I looked around, I didn't see anybody in sight. Finally, I located my car and rushed to unlock my door. Jumping into my car, I sped home scared and drove in silence. Once home, the living room light was still on. I quietly entered the doorway. I noticed something wasn't right. The door to the guest room my mother slept in once her divorce was final from my father was wide open.

Without making a sound, I took a peek to see if she was asleep. Instead, I heard the shower running with laughter, moaning, and cooing from the bathroom doorway. I wanted to die as I heard the two familiar voices. *My parents, no, this can't be, this can't be happening.*

While backing away from the door to avoid getting caught, I heard my mother moan intensely and call out my father's name. "Maxwell!"

I ran upstairs, freaking out as a kid. I wanted my parents to work on their marriage, but with my mother's rage and anger over me, I thought my father could do better, and I was glad they divorced. But why not tell me and keep this a secret from me. I had to get to the bottom of this, but I didn't want to get into my parents' business that I accidentally heard them having sex in the shower. As I tried to get over the situation and head for bed, I went to Erickson's room to kiss him goodnight. My little boy slept so peacefully as I rubbed his curly hair and kissed him on his cheeks. I decided that I would call the doctor Stacey recommended to me. I really needed to talk to someone. Maybe he can help me get through all this foolishness I've been through over the past five years. I opened Erickson's door and saw my father heading back to his room.

"Melinda, you scared me; I was in the study room." He held his rob tight. "I didn't know you got home."

"Yes, daddy, I was just checking on Erickson. I'm going to bed now." I kissed him on the cheek and closed my bedroom door. *Does my father think I'm stupid? He knows damn well; he wasn't in his damn study room!*

Chapter Seven

I woke up to the sounds of laughter coming from downstairs. So, I got dressed and went downstairs to find out about the excitement.

"Melinda, how are you?"

I was greeted with a hug from Donna.

"How are you, Donna?" I asked as I hugged her.

"I'm well. I just dropped by. Sorry about being late to see you back at home. But I came over to see you personally today, and now I am caught up on how your father is doing with his retirement. Also, I wanted to give you this," she gave me a small package. I opened it and saw a beautiful diamond tennis bracelet.

Looking at Donna, "This is beautiful," I said appreciatively and thanked her.

Donna waved her hand at me. "No worries, I mentioned to your father that the office isn't the same without you, and I have an offer for you. I hope that you will take it. I know you will be a great person for the job. Pamela and I discussed it, and we hope you will take my place and become Pamela's assistant. WHAT! I shouted. Donna smiled at my reaction.

"Melinda, you know the ropes, and we all respect you. Unfortunately, Pamela doesn't have time right now as she is working on a huge case to interview someone to take my place. I have to go away for a few days, and someone really needs to take my place on scheduling appointments."

After everything Donna did for me as my assistant, I had to pay her back by taking her offer. But I didn't want to step into that office and hear gossip about me. I made a mistake, and I paid the price. Besides, everyone showed up on my side during all my court hearings, so what could go wrong?

"Okay, Donna, when do I start?"

"I hope you can start tomorrow, but I figured you might need some time to get your mind situated on working again. Can you start early Monday morning?"

***

Monday morning came with a quickness. After dropping Erickson off at school, I drove to Maxwell Stone, Attorney at Law office building. I second-guessed myself, questioning if I should walk in or not. Then, taking a deep breath, I realized I had to do this for Donna. All eyes were on me as I entered my father's building. I didn't sweat it as I walked down the main hall; I knew every attorney who walked past me was clearly talking about me behind my back. But I didn't give a fuck.

I sat at Donna's desk and ran across papers of everyone's appointments from their clients and the thick calendar in front of me informing me who was having meetings or going somewhere for court. Then, as I was locating Pamela's schedule for the day, a familiar voice called my name.

"Ms. Melinda Stone, been a long time since I last saw you?"

I glanced up and saw Sheldon Mitchell.

"Hello, how are you? What are you doing here?" We embraced in a hug.

"Well, your girl Pamela hired me; she gave your boy a chance to be on the team, and I'm genuinely thankful."

"That's great, so how are they treating you here?"

"Well, you know how these folks in this office are always treating the newbies like their personal assistance till you let them know what you are all about... But, listen, Melinda, I heard what happened to you, and I am sorry you had to go through that."

"It's all good, Sheldon. I'm happy to be home, spending time with my family, getting to know my son, and hanging with my girls." Before we got into another conversation, the phone rang. "Well, let me get to work and take this call; let's catch up later?"

****

I didn't know how Donna did all this, sitting behind a desk: answering calls, filing papers, taking messages, and faxing. This was a lot of work. I am surprised she stuck around with my father and let alone me. It was almost 2:30 in the afternoon, and Pamela came to me. Tapping her long nails on the desk, "Let's go for lunch, my treat."

I smiled while stating I'd never decline a free meal. I grabbed my purse, and we headed to a new place downtown called The Chow. "Wow, a lot of new buildings have opened since I was locked up. I have missed out on a lot of things."

Pamela looked at me. "Nothing was popping out here when you were locked up Melinda, so don't trip. Besides, the girls and I really didn't go out much when you were in jail. It wasn't the same, not even for me. YOU KNOW I love when the four of us are out, and I'm sitting across from you, staring into your eyes. I gave out a smirk. "Pammie, stop," I said.

"WHAT?" Pamela said as she placed her right hand on my hand and touched the back of my hand. "I can't help but think about what happened the other night at your parents. It took me back to our college days." Our food arrived before things got steamy, and we ate and drank in silence.

Pamela paid for our meals, and we took a walk. We turned a corner around a building, and Pamela saw a sign, Ms. Glow Physic Reading. "Oh, Melinda, let's go inside. " Pamela cheesy begged like a kid in a candy store.

"Girl, I don't believe in this crazy physic reading shit."

"Come on. It will be fun," Pamela said, emphasizing she was paying for it.

She grabbed my hand, and we entered a dark, interiorly lit building. The place gave me the creeps. It had different pictures, and large tarot cards were posted on the walls. Let's get out of here now; I told Pamela. But, before I could get to the exit door, a woman came from behind the beads. She held her head down, only to lift her head and glance over to Pamela, addressing Pamela with a smile while greeting us.

"Welcome, ladies." Dismissing Pamela by looking at me and making eye contact. "Why are you so afraid, Melinda?" My mind screamed. What the fuck! How does she know my name? Dumbstruck and interested, I followed the woman to a seating area. She motioned for us to sit at a circular table with a deck of tarot cards. "I'm Miss. Glo, my service to you will be a hundred dollars." I had a bad feeling; I nudged Pamela, "Pammie, let's get out of here!"

Ignoring my request, "Please chill girl, and relax. What's the worst that can happen?" Pamela said.

"Seriously, Pamela, are you fucking serious?" I looked at the woman eyeing us.

Pamela smiled at the woman and talked to her directly while answering my question.

"Look, let me get my future read." Then, turning to me,

"And Melinda, if you change your mind, here is your fifty bucks to give her."

Pamela gave Ms. Glo her undivided attention. Ms. Glo began her reading as she cut the deck of cards in threes and had Pamela choose three face-down cards. Before looking at them, Ms. Glo did a blind reading and started talking before turning the cards over. Confirming the cards, she continued Pamela's reading. "You will have good fortune, but your love life is at a rocking point. You want to be with an old friend, but you don't know if that friend is as interested in you as you would like. You are working too hard; make time for yourself; don't put your work first, but balance work and leisure."

As Pamela got up, I saw tears in her eyes. I decided what the hell and decided to get a reading as well. I gave Ms. Glo fifty dollars and picked three cards from the deck. Unlike Pamela, Ms. Glo did not immediately start talking. She closed her eyes, then she opened them, and with a faraway look, she made one statement, "Melinda, would you like a refund?" I laughed, thinking it was a joke, and told her to go ahead and read what the cards said. Ms. Glo looked at me apprehensively, then started talking and confirmed the cards as she turned them over.

"Melinda, your past is coming back to haunt you. But the past is not -yet- to be continued-the revenge is not over death..."

I slammed my hands onto the table and told her to stop as I ran out; I didn't want to hear any more as I stormed out of the building and ran off. I could hear Pamela screaming my name, telling me to slow down. I ran past drivers blowing their horns at me for coming across the street. I got across to the other side and stopped to catch my breath with tears in my eyes. I was about to continue running when Pamela's car pulled up beside me and told me to get in.

"Leave me alone," I shouted. "I told you I wanted to leave and that I didn't want the physic reading done in the first place."

"Girl, you can believe or not believe in it I was just having fun. I'm sorry, Melinda, please get in the car."

As I got into the car, I said, "Take me home now, Pamela."

We drove in silence until Pamela asked, "What did Ms. Glo mean about your past is not yet to be continued."
I sighed, "I know what she meant, and another person does too."

"Who? What other person Melinda?" Pamela said.
I looked at her while she was driving as the heavy rain hit the front windshield of her car. "Otis Peterson ...."

Pamela came to a squeaking halt. She slammed her feet on the breaks so hard I thought we were going to crash. "What about him?" Pamela said as I touched her cheeks.

"I think I went to jail for the wrong reason; we both believe Erick Tyson isn't DEAD."

Pamela laughed so hard that I literally thought her head was about to explode. "You joking, right, Melinda? Please tell me you joking."

"Does it look like I'm joking? I believe, well, we believe Erick is still alive, and I want to find out the truth."

"You saw his lifeless body on your condo floor, and reports said he died at the scene, Pamela said.

"But what if it was all a lie? Erick knew a lot of people. What if someone lied on the documents. Remember the letters from Otis Peterson; he stated that he hired a private investigator, and there were no records, nothing on Erick, no burial, no cremation, nothing. Plus, he believes Kitty didn't kill herself. You got to believe me, Pamela. Then, out of nowhere, this physic woman tells me, well, you know. Plus, I never told you I had nightmares of being kidnapped by a man while in prison. He tied me up, and all I could see was him holding my son's hand, saying he got what he needed."

Pamela shook her head. "I swear that man in your dream sounds just like Erick. Melinda, you are serious about this," said Pamela.

As she started to continue, we got interrupted. We heard the sound of beeps from a car horn behind us and the driver screaming, telling us to move. We forgot we were in the middle of the road. Pamela drove me back to my parents. I couldn't help it; I knew I would be calling Otis in the morning.

"Listen, Melinda, get some rest, and I will make some phone calls and let you know what I come up with."

"Thanks Pamela."

***

After a day out, my mother greeted me by opening the door to the house.

"Do you realize you have a child in school, and you are coming home like this!" my mother shouted.

"Ma, I lost track of time I was with…" my mother cut in before I could finish.

"I don't give a damn who you were with; coming home at this time, you do realize whose home you are in, right? So, respect the rules, Melinda!"

Listening to her, after all I had experienced-something snapped.

"You know what, Ma? I've had this on my chest since I was a kid. Why do you hate me for the mistake you made? First, you cheated on daddy and got pregnant by another man. Then, you took all your wrongdoings and blamed them on me. Was it because Otis Peterson didn't want you, and he wasn't going to leave his wife?"

I felt the sting of pain on my cheek as I didn't see it coming. Looking at her, I rubbed where my mother slapped me. I wanted to hit my mother back so badly but didn't have the heart to do it. So instead, I spoke in a still voice with words to do the job. I was staring her down with my eyes.

"You are a pathetic woman," I chuckled as I finished my thoughts, shaking my head while looking at her.

"Like trash, Daddy should have thrown you out after hearing about your affair and then when the divorce was final."

"You bitch!" My mother shouted and reached for me, grabbing a handful of my hair as I turned to walk away. Pulling me by the hair, I yelled, "Let go. Let me go, you pathetic woman!"

My mother screamed, "No, you, you heifer! NO! Not in my house, Noooo!"

Hearing my mother and me, Maxwell ran out of his study room to break up our fight.

"My goodness, Martha, let her go! What has gotten into you all?"

Mother was straightening her appearance only to point at me.

"This disrespectful spoiled girl! Do you see the time? She just came home, Maxwell. She doesn't realize she has a child upstairs, and she wants to party all night with those trashy whores she calls her friends."

Maxwell looked at her. "Calm down, Martha. For God's sake, she is still trying to get herself together. Erickson is no problem. She lost five years of her life."

Martha rolled her eyes. "Oh, you are always taking up for this thing."

Maxwell looked at Martha, questioning, then glanced at me while pointing in my direction.

"This thing is your daughter. For God's sake, Martha, our daughter."

Looking at me, he called me by name. "Melinda go to bed, honey, please," said my father.

Looking at my Daddy, I spoke the words I didn't want to tell him.

"I can't take this anymore, Dad. Since my condo hasn't been sold, Erikson and I will be moving back there. So, I would like to know where all my belongings are to move back."

My father looked at me with determination and an edge in his voice.

"No, Melinda! I won't allow you to live in that condo. You are fine here!"

My mother chuckled and said, "Let her go."

Maxwell turned his eyes on my mother. Then, quietly stating, "Martha, hush!"

I really took in the whole scene, and I wanted answers.

"Daddy, I know I was innocent, but why take me in as your own, raising another man's child? You divorced mommy, and still, she is here. Why?"

My father sat in his chair, looking a little older than he did moments ago, while he rubbed his temples. "You needed a father, baby, and I am not the man who would abandon an innocent child." While looking at my mother, "I knew I wasn't a father to our son. I work a lot to keep my business. It is what I created; it is solid. I hope you forgive me for that. When you got pregnant with Melinda, I wanted to show you I was a good man. So, I got a second chance to be a father again." As tears trickled down my face, my mother walked over to my father and planted a kiss on his forehead. I couldn't resist asking at that moment.

"Are the two of you back together?"

"We are working through this, Melinda. I forgave your mother, and that's all you should know. "

"But that is not what I asked Daddy."

"Why does that matter, Melinda? We are both adults and handle our personal life privately. We don't have to discuss our private life with you, Melinda," shouted my mother.

Still feeling some way towards my mother, I couldn't hold my peace. Years of not being loved can do that to a child.

"Well, Ma, if it was so private, next time while you two are screwing one another in the guestroom shower, lock both doors, the bathroom, and the guestroom," I said as I stormed upstairs to my room.

***

I woke up at six-thirty in the morning, got Erickson ready for school, and headed to the law firm. As I drove looking for a parking space, I saw my old parking space was taken by Pamela. She has my office. Damn, she could have let a bitch keep her parking space.

****

Damn, what happened to your face? I heard as I looked up and there stood Pamela.

"Mother and daughter smackdown last night. Father broke it up."

"Melinda, are you serious?"

"Yeah, thanks to you."

While we walked into Maxwell Law Firm, Pamela confirmed my inner thoughts. "You were right, Melinda."

"Right about what?"

"Erick's body is a mystery, and I called several people I knew. Unfortunately, they have no knowledge of a deceased body with the name Erick Tyson. But it still doesn't make him alive, Melinda. We have to investigate, and if he is still alive, we have to play this the right way and let the police get involved. I still have several people that haven't gotten back to me. So, let us wait until I hear their feedback. Then we can plan to handle the next step, okay?"

I nodded and told Pamela I would be taking an early lunch break. I reached for my phone and dialed Otis Peterson's number. He picked up on the fourth ring. I heard the strange man's voice on the phone repeatedly saying hello, who is this. Finally, I got the courage to speak and said, this is Melinda Stone; we need to talk. I gave Otis the location for us to meet, a coffee shop a few blocks from the office. Luckily, he was in my hometown on business and today was his last day here. He decided to cancel his plane ticket and spend an extra day. I waited for Otis to arrive. I ordered a hazelnut coffee; as I took another sip from my cup, a man approached me with flowers.

"Melinda, this is for you," it was Otis Peterson.

"Thank you, but you shouldn't have, as I placed the flowers in the empty seat next to me. Otis sat across from me.

"You look so beautiful," said Otis. "I'm glad you called me. I know I'm the last man you would want to have a conversation with, but I didn't mean to abandon you. It's just that I didn't know what I was thinking. At that point, I was already married with kids, and I cheated on my wife while she was battling cancer. I knew I was wrong, and I hope you find it in your heart to forgive me, Melinda."

Otis placed his hand on mine. "I hope we can get to know one another and have a father and daughter relationship, only at your pace. I see that your mother took very good care of you," I cut Otis off.

"My mother didn't do shit, thanks to you. She treated me like I was a damn orphan kid. My mother hated me since that day when I was a little girl, and she spotted you, wanting to let you know I existed. But when you turned your back on us, she turned her back on me. I'm truly grateful for my father, Maxwell Stone, who stepped in and gave me the love I needed and taught me everything I needed to know."

I snatched my hand from Otis and cleared my throat.

"Mr. Peterson, I am not here to discuss a family bond. I grew past that a long time ago. You chose who you wanted and closed the door on those who also needed you." The waiter came up and took Otis's order, and he began to talk again.

"My wife found out about you. My daughter told her the day before she died. She visited us with a folder demanding answers to what I had been hiding all these years. I had to tell the truth. I couldn't lie. All the facts were right there in that folder, including a DNA test."

"WHAT?!" I almost choked on my coffee. "I never consented to a DNA test," I said.

"I know you didn't, Ms. Stone, but somehow Erick got a hold of our DNA and ran the test. It came back that you are my daughter."

My inner thoughts were raging. That bastard was living with me to get back on his feet. And right under my nose stole my DNA, and I didn't know it. Damn! Erick was smarter than I thought.

I came out of my thoughts to hear Mr. Peterson continuing his life issues. "So, my wife, she divorced me. My sons were angry, and they stopped talking to me. My wife left me, and with that, she took everything. I couldn't blame her. I cheated. I lied and got another woman pregnant, and I thought nobody would find out about you. Victoria stormed out, and that was the last time I heard from her. A couple of days later, I saw on the news that my daughter had killed herself. I know that's a lie. That's why I decided to contact you. Your information was on your business card. I convinced your receptionist to give me the address to your home. I wrote you letters, but I thought you were avoiding me when you didn't contact me after sending six letters. Then I saw on the front page of the newspaper that you were found guilty of murdering Erick Tyson. Both my daughters were in trouble, and I didn't do anything. This time I'm willing to help one. I hope that Victoria would be proud of me for solving her case, and in turn, for both of you, that asshole Erick gets what he deserves, which is to be buried beneath the jail. Overlooking your dislike for me, I am begging you. I need your help, Melinda. Please help me…"

I heard his grief and disgust for Erick and thought, what am I supposed to do? "I feel you, Mr. Peterson, and we agree on what is right. Since we are being open…" I told Otis about Ms. Glo, the psychic, and all she implied. He was in more shock than I was.

"You need to be careful, Melinda. There's no point right now going to the police without the proper evidence." Otis reached down, opened a briefcase, and pulled out some folders. "Here is everything I have. Hopefully, we can put all the missing pieces together. I'll let you go over this and make arrangements to revisit you. Right here, okay?" I looked at him as he continued, not waiting for an answer. Let me know what you come up with; he waved to the waiter, paid for our coffee, said his goodbye, and walked out.

Chapter Eight

"The phone has been ringing off the hook'" said Sheldon, "but don't worry, I covered for you."

"Thanks, now you can go and let me get back to my work," I said.

Sheldon noticed my hands, "It looks like you've been already working, as he pointed to the folders in my hands. "Ms. Stone, I believe you miss this, don't you?"

"This isn't what you think it is," I chuckled.

"Well, if you need a helping hand, don't be a stranger. I'm here to lend my services," said Sheldon.

Smiling, I pointed at him. "You know what, maybe I do need your help. Can you stop by Pamela's office and tell her to stay behind after everyone leaves? I would like the both of you to meet me in the conference room."

Happy with the turn of events, Sheldon smiled and said, "Will do."

***

Sheldon, and Pamela, looked at me.

"Oh, come on, Melinda, this is my Friday," as she saw the folders in my hand. "No more cases," said Pamela.

Sheldon laughed at her. "Let's just see what she got."

Pamela gave him a look that could kill. He raised his hands as if to surrender and smiled.

I sighed and looked at Pamela, "Listen, I know it's Friday, but this one is important. So, take a seat."

Pamela eyed me like this better be good. Sheldon sat interested and happy to be in on something.

"I met up with Otis Peterson, and he gave me these folders. He states that his daughter Victoria Peterson aka Kitty, didn't kill herself; he also doesn't believe Erick is dead either," I said.

Confused and stunned, Sheldon blurted out, "Excuse me, who is Erick and this Otis and Kitty?"

"Damn it. I forgot we got to fill you in."

Sheldon got the 411, and I showed them the DNA test. Both were speechless. Sheldon rubbed his hand across his face. "DAMN!" Erick, a bad mutherfucker if he is still alive, needs to be on our team," Sheldon said.

"SHUT-UP!" we both screamed in unison at Sheldon.

"Damn, this is fucked up on so many levels, but let's get to work," said Pamela.

Reading Otis's notes and what the private investigator wrote, the three of us put our heads together and went to work.

"Melinda, have you contacted anybody Erick knew since you've been out of prison?" Sheldon asked.

"No, I didn't... wait a minute, I did. I spoke with Stacey."

Pamela, surprised, loudly said, "You did WHAT? When was this?"

Sheldon sensing a change in the atmosphere, brought us back to attention. "Ladies, chill out, and who is Stacey?"

Still a little hot, Pamela stated, "Erick's side piece, or was you the side piece, and she the girlfriend? Either way, he was playing you both."

"Really, Pamela, that's how you are going to put it. A slap in my face by throwing my business out like that? It wasn't like it was intentional. I met her at Sasha's after-church event. Erikson and I stayed to help feed the homeless. While taking out the trash, I saw her with some people down the road. She came over and thanked me for getting her probation, and apologized for what had happened. She even confessed that she had changed her life, got clean, and was married. Also, she gave me a business card for a recommended counselor. But I haven't made an appointment. One thing I remember, as Erickson and I departed to go home, in my rearview mirror, I noticed that she was arguing with someone on the phone."

Pamela chuckled. "That could have been Erick."

"We don't know that. But do we have Stacey's contact information," said Sheldon.

"Nope," I said.

"She is not stupid to give you that," stated Pamela.

"Well, damn, we're back at square one," said Sheldon. "Do you think we can get a search warrant and look through Ms. Victoria's call logs? Also, if we can, get another order to view her body with the approval of her father to get another autopsy done. Then, once we get all this arranged, we can go from there."

Sheldon looked at the clock on the wall. "Melinda, it's getting late. Let's call this a night."

We all agreed, got our things, and left the office.

****

The phone rang loudly, disturbing Travis Freeman, one of Sheldon's frat brothers. Looking at the caller ID, it was an unknown number. Travis answered.

A man with a raspy voice spoke. "Well, well, well, if it isn't my cousin minister Travis Freeman, word on the block says you have a frat brother, officially a lawyer and working at my known enemy's firm, Maxwell Law."

Travis was irritated with the voice on the other end. "Who the fuck is this?"

The raspy-voiced man said, "Nigga you know who the fuck this is. I thought you were all about family and taking action with what happened to Silk. But, dealing with the mutherfuckers who were involved in his death, your bitch ass must have had a change of heart and turned against your fucking family."

"Listen, Erick; I don't want to get into this crazy shit you got going on. But, yeah, I have a college buddy who's been more than just a friend to me. And yes, he does work at Maxwell law firm. So why do you need me- I'm not fucking up what he is building for that company."

Erick chuckled, "You will be dealing with a lot more if you don't step up your game. I want to destroy that company and the family. Blood is thicker than water, in case you forgot about that shit. Besides, your frat fuck brother isn't what you thought he was. I know some shady shit you don't know."

"What the fuck are you talking about," shouted Travis.

"Well, when your ass got locked up for that drug and possession of a weapon charge, the one you served three years in jail."

"Yeah, I remember," said Travis.

"Your bitch that you thought would hold it down for you, Monica. Well, while you were locked up, your bitch was fucking your boy, Sheldon. The bitch got pregnant, and who you think is the fucking father."

"Man, get the fuck outta here, you lying."

"Both was playing you, cuz. Why would I lie to you about this when I knew you were in love with that bitch," said Erick.

Feeling the vibe from Travis, Erick continued. "So, your bitch ass doesn't believe me, well go see for yourself. She is located on Fourth Street at this apartment complex called River Bay. I believe she lives in apartment F23. When you get your proof, you know where to find me to continue with what we fucking started, burning the Stone's family to the ground."

Travis was confused and lost, but he knew Erick would never lie to him about anything. He knew his cousin always had his best interest at heart, and the Stone family had to pay for what happened to Silk. So, Travis took matters into his own hands and drove to where Monica was apparently located. As he drove, he reminisced about meeting Monica at a bar. Even though things moved relatively fast for them, they fell in love. Monica wasn't the type you could take home to your mother. She was a head buster, a go-getter, the type of bitch where if you fucked her up by any means, you would get dealt with.

But whatever Monica did was her business. She was all about getting money; anyway, she could, no matter the situation. A tragic accident caused Monica to change her life, and even though she had her faults, Travis was there by her side, helping her get back on her feet. Travis loved Monica and wanted to settle down with her and start a family. Travis trusted Monica, and when he got locked up, he trusted Monica to be faithful - holding it down till he got out. Travis entrusted her with his savings of fourteen thousand dollars located in a safe. He told Monica to keep the money until he came home so they could build on their future together.

After Travis went away, Monica went on a shopping spree with everything Travis had. When the money was gone, Monica lied and told Travis she had got robbed and everything was taken, including all the money he had saved in his safe. While in jail, there was nothing Travis could do, but he believed Monica while watching the tears smear her made-up face. Once Monica knew that Travis believed her lying scheme, she packed up, took along some of Travis's jewelry, and left town. Monica met Sheldon.

Sheldon knew Travis dated Monica, but he thought it wasn't that serious between them. Then, after several one-night stands occurring between them, Monica found out she was pregnant.

Sheldon took responsibility to help support her and their baby. But they agreed not to let Travis find out about them and that the relationship had gotten her pregnant.

Speeding down the road, Travis was thinking so hard, hoping that Erick was lying about his best friend fucking his lady behind his back, especially when he was locked up. Travis entered the complex to Monica's crib and had second thoughts about knocking on the door. But he wanted to know the truth. It had been a long time, and Travis wanted answers. Why did Monica up and vanish as she did when she told him -she would wait for him until he got released.

Travis banged on the door; a little girl with curly black hair opened the door holding a chocolate chip cookie in her hand. She smiled and said, "Hello, can I help you?" Travis stared into the girl's eyes, and without even trying, he knew this little girl was Sheldon's. A female voice came from the back, "Who's at the door, baby?"

"I don't know, mommy," shouted Kayla. Travis knew exactly who the voice belonged to.

As Monica approached the front door and saw who was on the other side, the glass in Monica's hand dropped and shattered on the floor. "Travis, what are you doing here?"

"I came for the truth, and found it, you little bitch! You stole from me, took everything I had, and got pregnant with Sheldon's baby while I was locked up!?" Travis wanted so badly to put his hands around Monica's neck and choke her till she took her last breath. But he knew that was wrong, especially seeing Monica's daughter screaming inside the apartment.

"Don't yell at my mommy!"

"Please, Travis, I'm sorry for what I did. Please forgive me. I made a terrible mistake. I didn't mean to hurt you."

***

Sheldon pulled his car into a parking space with flowers and a gift for his daughter. When he arrived at Monica's apartment, he was greeted with a surprise from Travis. Before getting a word out, Travis punched Sheldon in the jaw. Both men fought as Monica screamed for them to stop. It took two men from another apartment to break apart Sheldon and Travis.

"We supposed to be boys, and you go behind my back and fuck my girl. As Travis pushed the man who was holding him from attacking Sheldon. After wiping the blood from his busted lip, staring at Monica with an evil look in his eyes, he said one word, "BITCH", and stormed off to call Erick.

Little Kayla ran outside to greet her daddy with a hug and gently rubbed her father's swollen jaw. "That's a bad man," said Kayla to Sheldon.

"I know, baby girl." Sheldon grabbed the damaged box with Kayla's gift and handed it to her. She ran into the house to see what her daddy had brought.

"How the fuck did he know where you lived," shouted Sheldon to Monica.

"I don't know; I never told anybody where I live. Why would I mess up when you're paying all the bills here, Sheldon? I wouldn't do you like that."

"You know what, I need to stop fucking with you and just focus on my daughter." Sheldon looked on the ground; flower petals were everywhere. Then, looking at Monica and not wanting to stay longer, "I can't believe this shit." Sheldon turned away from her, walked to his car, and drove off.

128

Chapter Nine

I pulled out the card I had received from Stacey as I waited for the receptionist to call me back for my appointment. *Now was a good time to meet this doctor; brushing everything off wasn't doing me any good. I have to talk to someone, and these dreams are so stressful. I'm tired of being restless.* So, I sat on the sofa discussing my problem with Dr. Lewis. He jotted notes on a notebook pad, and I thought I was going crazy discussing my problems with a stranger. But it felt good talking to a professional about my problems.

"Do you feel like your life is in danger Melinda?"

"I really don't know Dr. Lewis, but I feel like my past is out to haunt me."

"Melinda, I'm going to write you a prescription for stress and for you to sleep better. Okay, and I'd like to schedule a follow-up visit to discuss your life changes and experiences and see how the medications work to help you through the issues you discussed. With all that you have shared, you also need to get out more and enjoy life with your son and family."

I walked out of Dr. Lewis's office with the two prescriptions in my hand. I knew I wasn't crazy. I balled up the paper and threw it in the trash. Then, I walked to my car and headed home. My father was in the kitchen as he called me, telling me I had a letter from the women's prison. A big smile spread across my face; it was Money. I rushed upstairs to my room, ran a hot bath, and read Money's letter.

Melinda,
Hey, baby, I miss you so much. Since you've been gone, things haven't been the same. I refused to get a new cellmate; your bed still lay untouched since your release. I wish you were with me many nights when I kissed and pleased your body. I love the way you tasted and felt. Since you left and told me that you love me, I love you too. I have some good news to share. I will be going to another court hearing. I hope to have my sentence shortened if it happens, baby; we can be together. We can be a family. I can't wait to see you again, baby, and make sweet love to you. While you wrap your legs on my shoulder as I eat your pussy till you cum back-to-back on my tongue.
Take care boo. I hope to hear from you soon
love,

Money

Reading Money's letter gave me goosebumps. I missed her so much. I never thought I would enjoy nor fall in love with a woman all over again. As I played with my pussy in the tub, caressing my throbbing pointy nipples, I imagined that Money was in the tub with me. My hands were her hands as she played with my pussy. I moaned, splashing water onto the floor. I fingered my pussy harder and deeper. To finger fucking myself better, I put my leg on the edge of both sides of the tub, pushing my body in the tub.

My hands at play felt so good while fantasizing about Money, and reminiscing on our lovemaking made me even hornier. But before I could explode, my cell phone rang. The phone vibration scared me so much my entire head almost slid under the water. I picked up on the third rung. Nobody was on the other end of the line as I repeatedly said hello.

Once I hung up and placed the phone back on the toilet seat, I continued where I left off. Again, before opening my legs- my cell phone rang again. I should have looked at who was calling me but instead shouted, "HELLO, STOP PLAYING ON MY DAMN PHONE!"

"Relax, damn, who pissed you off?"

I knew who the other caller was. It was Pamela. "Sorry girl, wassup?"

"I was checking up on you, had you on my mind, and wanted to see if I could come over."

"Pamela, we can't be doing this; eventually, we're going to get caught," I said as my throbbing pussy needed some relief. "Okay, fine, I'll let you inside."

Pamela and I made love all night, and we lay naked, cuddling each other. My body was at ease before I closed my eyes to sleep. I couldn't help but think about who I wanted to be with; I had known Pamela since we were kids. But after being locked up with Money for five years, I caught mad feelings for her too. What if Money gets released early, finds me, and wants me to spend my life with her? I was confused and had to decide, but how could that happen when I'm in love with both women. Early in the morning, I woke up, went downstairs, and greeted my mother as she put breakfast on the table.

"Good morning, mother." Not speaking, she looked me up and down and went back into the kitchen to bring out the rest of the food and beverages. My father came out of his studies and greeted me with a kiss on my forehead. Erickson and Pamela came rushing downstairs, racing to the table.

"Something sure smells good, Grandma Martha," Erickson said.

"Good morning, Pamela; glad to see you again; how is everything going," said my father.

Pamela hugged him before sitting down. We sat quietly eating breakfast in silence, hearing the silverware clinking against the glass plates. Suddenly my mother, out of nowhere, disturbed the silence.

"Melinda, when are you planning to get a man; get out on your own you know this boy needs a father?" I rolled my eyes and pretended that I didn't hear her question. She repeated it. "Melinda, did you hear me? When are you planning to get a man and get out on your own; this boy needs a father?"

"Are you serious right now? Can I eat breakfast in peace?"

"No man has called nor came over here to take you out. Therefore, you must be a lesbian."

Pamela choked on a piece of bacon. At the same time, I tried to get up and leave. Instead, my father pushed me back down to finish breakfast. I sat and then found my voice to speak.

"I have been through so much these past years. I don't want a man, not now, not after...," I looked at Erickson and paused my thoughts. "I'm focusing on myself and my son."

My mother went into a fit. "No daughter of mine is not going to be a damn...!"

Cutting my mother off, "Oh! So, I'm your daughter now after all these years. I'm finally your child. Mother, you are something else." Interrupting my final thoughts to give to my mother, Pamela excused herself from the table.

"Melinda, I think it's best I leave now. I will see you at the office, and I'll make sure to inform Sheldon to stay over so we can finish where we left off. I enjoyed breakfast."

***

"I can't believe your mother this morning. You know you're welcome to stay at my place whenever you need some time to get away. It will bring us closer together, Pamela said as she gave me a wink."

"I'll be fine."

"Good morning, ladies."

"DAMN, what happened to you, Sheldon?" Pamela and I noticed his black eye and bruised cheeks.

"I don't want to talk about it."

"Glad you have office call meetings and not heading to court with that eye," I said.

"Very funny. I'll see you later." Sheldon walked down the hall, following Pamela to her office, and closed the door behind him. It was a relief when the phone calls finally stopped coming in. My ears needed a break from talking to clients. I wanted to go home, but Sheldon and Pamela were waiting for me in the conference room to finish the mystery of whether Erick was dead or alive.

"Melinda, I don't know where to start; we are still at square one."

"Pamela, I don't know what to do either? Should I give up?"

"No, you shouldn't give up. I think you should contact that lady, maybe roughen her up, get drinks, and maybe she will slip up and tell you something you need to know," said Sheldon.

"I think that's a good idea, Sheldon. Melinda, maybe you should get in touch with Stacey. Let's see if she was up in Erick's ass doing crazy things. You never know what could come out of her mouth. It's a start, Melinda," said Pamela. "Just try it out."

Pamela looked at her watch. "Let's call it an early night. I have a critical meeting in the morning. Is there anything else? Sheldon and I agreed it was an excellent place to stop and call it a night. I agreed it had been a day and an early night to get home, and rest sounded good.

"Well, I need to rest up. Catch you guys later." We said goodbye to Pamela as she left the conference room.

Sheldon looked at Melinda. He wasn't ready to call it a night. "Melinda, do you want to go out for a drink?"

"Not tonight, Sheldon, rain check? I'm pretty tired too, and I better get home."

"Come on, Melinda, you owe me."

I looked at him like he was crazy. "Owe you for what?"

Sheldon chuckled. "For Costa Rica, you owe me, knowing what I know now and how you acted towards me."

"Okay, fine, I was a bit rude to you, but only one drink."

Sheldon and I went to a bar and had shots after shots as we listened to spoken word from various poetic artists. Sheldon was a great listener, and he made me laugh all night. I realized Sheldon wasn't the type to hold his liquor. After the last three shots, Sheldon was a total waste. I walked and supported Sheldon to get to his car. Luckily Sheldon's place wasn't far from the law firm. I thought about my car as I drove Sheldon's.

I'll help him to bed, take the late bus to the office, and drive home.

But Sheldon begged me to stay a little bit longer as we sat down to watch a comedy show on television. I looked at the time; it was almost midnight.

"I really need to get going, Sheldon."

Not sure he heard me, I watched as Sheldon moved next to me and gently pulled my hair away, exposing my neck. Why wasn't I moving to leave?

Sheldon kissed me at the base of my neck. The alcohol on his breath hit my nostril, and it didn't bother me as he softly caressed my neck with kisses. Sheldon undid each button down the front of my shirt and trailed kisses.

I answered my question; It felt so different to finally feel the touch of a man since the last touch was Erick. As he reached my bra, I bit my bottom lip and gave out a soft moan in anticipation. Then, he lifted and exposed my breast to gently suck on my swollen nipples as his warm tongue made circles on my areola. Sheldon lifted my skirt, spread my legs, and I raised my ass. He removed my thong, and my pussy got wetter in expectation. *I hope Sheldon knows how to fuck; it has been five long years since I had a dick,* I thought.

Instead, Sheldon pulled me close and placed my legs on his shoulders. Sheldon's tongue game wasn't impressive.

GREAT! This muthafucker doesn't know how to lick the clit. If he would only shut the fuck up while trying

to eat my pussy. Sheldon talked over and over, asking how did I like it. Then, he licked the tip of my clit like a kitten with a warm bowl of milk. I really wanted Sheldon to stop; he was embarrassing himself badly. I can't tell Pamela about this. I felt more of Sheldon's saliva running between my legs than his fucking tongue. This was some straight bullshit, and in my mind, I was questioning *where my underwear and skirt* were because it was time to go! *Sheldon unzipped his pants, and my pussy was throbbing so badly that I didn't move, and I didn't know if Sheldon had put on a condom. All thoughts were gone except one word.*
DAMN.

Sheldon's dick was thick with a curve as he entered my tight pussy. I almost wanted him to stop as he pulled my legs around his waist and went deeper into me, roughly fucking me on his couch. My juices ran down my thighs as Sheldon's dick rhythmically slid against my walls. I held onto the back of Sheldon's couch. Damn, his dick felt amazing inside me. My pussy throbbed with each deep stroke. My walls tightened and gripped his long massive curved dick until he moaned. I didn't know which was better fucking me from the front or the back. Sheldon bent me over, and damn, I swear Sheldon's dick kept growing and growing inside of me.

"Fuck me, Sheldon, oh fuck me!" I screamed. Sheldon smacked me on my ass cheeks as the stings got a little painful; it turned me on.

"Damn, you got some good ass pussy, Melinda!" Sheldon pulled out, and I repositioned before he could say get on top. I rode him like a bull as Sheldon grabbed my breasts, sucking my nipples. I couldn't control myself.

Sheldon's dick felt so good. Sheldon repositioned, moving behind me; he bent me over the armrest of his couch and drove his dick deep into my pussy fucking me from behind. I felt each long deep stroke, and I reared back to meet each stroke until he was pounding into my pussy. Finally, Sheldon pulled out and released a massive amount of cum on the middle part of my back. I felt it trickling down. Sheldon rushed to his bathroom and got a towel to clean me up. I looked at the clock on Sheldon's wall; it was three in the morning.

"Damn Sheldon, look at the time I got to go."

"Let me take you to get your car. "

"No, Sheldon, you are drunk. I can take the bus or call a cab to get my car. I'll send you a text to let you know that I made it home."

***

My mother caught me coming inside the house while she came out of my dad's room. Before she closed his door, I glanced in at my father's mirror and saw him fast asleep.

"Melinda, look what time it is."

My mother knew the look in my eyes that I knew what had happened again with her and my father. Having a change in thought, she said goodnight and headed to the guest room.

I checked on Erickson and saw he was asleep. Then I went to my room and closed the door and laughed. Guess we both got some dick this morning, I thought; I took a shower and went to bed.

***

"How would you like to have a permanent position," Pamela asked.

"Good morning, Pamela. What are you talking about?"

"Well, I just got off the phone with Donna, and she is not coming back. Before you get all hassled about it. Melinda, you need this job. Your mother is a trip, and wouldn't you like to have your own place again, now that you have Erickson?"

I needed the job like I needed the money, but being at my father's law firm wasn't in my plans. I only returned doing a favor for Donna, and now she is not coming back? This was so stressful.

"Fine, Pamela, I will stay, but soon you will have to find another receptionist."

"Well, hello, ladies. Good morning, Melinda," said Sheldon as he walked past us into his office. Taking a second look, he couldn't help himself; he looked at me directly with a smile. My legs started to shake; luckily, nobody noticed when Sheldon licked his lips after shutting the door behind him. My pussy cooed to have his dick again.

Pamela chuckled. "What was that all about?"

I shrug my shoulders, "I really don't know."

Every time Sheldon saw me, he flirted. My phone line was ringing off the hook. I thought they were clients, but it was Sheldon asking me to come into his office or just to bring him coffee. Each time I entered, Sheldon would lock his door, bend me over the chair in front of his desk and fuck me so damn good I knew why I hate having quickies.

It took me a while to climax, and Sheldon would bust a nut almost as soon as he slid in his dick. Unfortunately, we would have to stop as we were afraid of getting caught.

After the fourth time entering Sheldon's office, I had to but didn't want to inform him that we couldn't do this at work. He insisted that I come over tonight.

"I can't Sheldon. I have plans tonight."

He brushed himself against my ass. "Are you sure you want to turn down this long dick Melinda? "

"Okay fine, I'll think of something."

My lunch break was near, and I told Pamela I had a few errands, and I might come back late since today was a slow day. So, she let me have the rest of the day off. I text Sheldon.

I will be waiting at your place.

He had already been out of the office and on his lunch break. We didn't hesitate. Sheldon lifted my skirt and started fucking me hard and deep. We finally got to his bedroom, where we fucked like wild animals. The sweat on Sheldon's bald head dripped from his head to my lips as I wiped his sweat with the palm of my hands and held onto his waist with my legs. Something wasn't right. Sheldon was getting aggressive with my body to the point I wanted him to stop. But his dick was getting so good, but my pussy was finally at her breaking point. I was getting sore, and Sheldon still hadn't nutted. I tried to pull him off me, but with him being stronger, I finally had to tell him.

"Sheldon, please stop." Not hearing me as he was getting so aggressive that I screamed so loudly. "SHELDON, PLEASE, STOP!"

"Why did you have to hurt me, Monica? Take this dick, take it just like you like it rough."

"MONICA! Who the fuck is Monica?"

Sheldon finally came to his senses. When he realized I was Melinda and not Monica, a couple more pounding inside my walls, Sheldon erupted all inside me. What was supposed to be good became a nightmare. When Sheldon got off me, I was sitting in a large bloodstain. I touched my sore pussy and lifted my hand. My fingertips were covered with my blood.

"WHAT THE FUCK, SHELDON? What did you do to me? "I tried to get up but was too sore to move.

"Melinda, I'm sorry I don't know what came over me."

"So now you know my name. You were just calling me some bitch named Monica."

Confused, Sheldon looked so ashamed and dropped his head. "Melinda, please forgive me. Let me help clean you up."

"Stop, don't fucking touch me," as I crawled out of Sheldon's bed, searching for my cellphone in which I missed a few calls from Tasha's ass.

Tears dropped from my eyes onto my cheeks. The pain was too much to take. Tasha called me the fourth time, and I picked up, trying not to cause a huge scene on the phone.

"Yes, Tasha, sorry I missed your call, wassup girl." I did the best I could to sound like I wasn't in so much pain, but I couldn't help it. Tasha picked up on my voice. I didn't sound like my usual self.

"Girl, what is wrong with you? You better not lie."

"I got to go to the hospital, Tasha. I'm in so much pain."

"Hospital, okay, something has to be wrong; you rarely get sick?" asked Tasha.

"Look, I'll explain later, but I'm leaving to head there now."

"Let me swing by to pick you up, and I will go with you, so you won't have to be alone, Melinda?"

Great, Tasha, ghetto ass, will never keep this shit to herself. If she could, she would broadcast my business on Facebook live.

"Melinda, please. I am so sorry; let me help you to your car?"

"Who's that in the background?!" shouted Tasha.

Damn, Tasha heard Sheldon's voice in the background. I raised my finger to my lip to inform him to shut up.

"Tasha, I'll be there to get you." I hung up quickly before I heard another word from her. Sheldon was panicking and apologizing so heavily as I got all the strength in my sore body to get out of the bed. I grabbed the towel off Sheldon's laundry basket and put on my skirt. I wouldn't dare try to put back on my thong, and I stormed out of Sheldon's apartment.

***

"What's going on, Melinda," Tasha said as she slammed the door to my car.

"What the fuck? Why are you sitting on a damp towel?"

"If you shut up, Tasha, and let me answer one question at a time, I will tell you," I said as I sped to the hospital. I told Tasha everything. First, she laughed, then bounced in the seat, singing to her ghetto ass self.

"He beat the pussy cat up up up up," as she clapped her hands together.

"Girl, if I weren't in so much pain, I would slap you right now. And Tasha, please don't run your fucking big mouth to nobody about this."

"I won't say anything, Melinda. You have my word." Tasha got out and got me a wheelchair. I signed myself in, and luckily, I was rushed back to a room. The doctors and nurses ran tests and ultimately did their best to stop the bleeding. Doctor Ellen Grant explained what happened and gave me medication. "Remember to give your vagina time to heal Ms. Stone and no sex for a few weeks."

"You don't have to worry about anything, doctor. I'm done fucking with that bastard."

Tasha drove back to her place. I texted my father and told him I would be staying at Tasha's. I lied and told him I felt dizzy and couldn't drive home. I was glad my father wasn't the type to ask many questions. I texted Pamela that I wouldn't be able to come to work in the morning; she was curious to know what was going on. Damn, I wish my friends weren't into my fucking business. Sheldon was blowing my phone up like crazy. All I wanted was one day off to relax, soak my sore pussy in a hot tub of water, then relax with my son afterward. But as life would have it. I wouldn't enjoy one day off till the weekend started. I didn't make it to my desk to put down my belongings before Sheldon's retarded ass came flying at me.

"I hope you forgive me, Melinda. I don't know what came over me the other day."

"Sheldon, I forgive you but know that you will never get a piece of this pussy ever again. Go back to the woman you called Monica and destroy her walls the way you did mine."

"Melinda, it's not like that, I'm feeling you, and if you give me another chance, I promise that side won't come out. I will never hurt you. I enjoy making love to you. I can't get enough of how your pussy feels on my dick," said Sheldon.

"Am I interrupting something here? My mouth dropped as I looked up and there stood Sasha. Satan is really riding my ass. The pastor's wife, who happens to be my friend, heard Sheldon's conversation with me. "Sasha, I didn't see you standing there. What are you doing here? What you heard; it is not like that."

Sasha raised her hands to shut me up. "I don't judge Melinda. I leave that up to God. I'm here to take my friends out to lunch. But I may need to reschedule."

"No, Sasha, it's fine; he was just leaving," as I gave Sheldon an evil look to get the fuck on before he tried to introduce himself to Sasha.

"Pamela isn't here; she's in court," I said.

"I know," replied Sasha, "and Tasha is out of town, so it will just be us two."

We went to a quiet little lounge and waited for our food to arrive at our table. "I haven't seen you in a while. How is everything," I said to Sasha.

"Everything is going well; I had some good news to share with you, Tasha, and Pamela, but they will have to find out later. My husband wanted to keep it to ourselves for a while, but I told him I had to share it with my girlfriends. So, he insisted that afterward, I could not tell anyone else," Sasha explained. As I waited for Sasha to spill the exciting news, our food came out.

"Well, Melinda, I'm pregnant ...."

"What, are you serious? Congrats, you and Nick are going to be great parents!"

"Praise Jesus, the lord has finally answered our prayers," Sasha said as she rubbed her belly.

Lunch was good, but I had to let Sasha know I had to hurry back to the office. We walked out to the car, and the area looked so familiar. We walked farther, almost to the parking area where Sasha parked her car. There stood the open sign hanging on the door to Miss. Cleo, I told Sasha I had to make a stop. Shook up and scared, I opened the door to enter.

"Melinda, I don't feel right about this," stated Sasha.

"It's you again, Melinda," as Miss. Cleo came from the back. "I knew you would come back, and I see you brought a new friend. Hello, did you come to get your fortune read?"

"The only person who knows my fortune is my Jesus lord and savior," stated Sasha as she turned to me. "Melinda, if you are up to this, I'll see you in the car," and walked out the door.

Miss Cleo motioned me to sit down. "Melinda, give me your hands and relax."

Miss Cleo closed her eyes and squeezed my hands in hers. "Are you ready for what I'm about to tell you?" A large lump was in my throat, I barely couldn't get the word yes out, so I nodded that I was ready for what she was about to tell me.

"Melinda, your past is getting so strong you are still in danger. They are out for blood, your blood, your family's blood. You need to leave town, but you will still be found if you leave. I see a woman who is hurt badly, and the police won't come in time to save her. This woman has a strong connection to you."

"OH NO! Is it PAMELA," I shouted?

Miss Cleo continued, "I see a little boy screaming for his mother as he was being taken away." I snatch my hands from Cleo's hands and jump out of the chair. "Nobody is going to hurt my son," I shouted with tears in my eyes. Then, I dug deep in my purse and pulled out a fifty-dollar bill.

"It's on the house," said Miss. Cleo. "Melinda, be careful and stop by tomorrow. I'll have a charm necklace ready for you, and it will protect you." I stormed out, running as fast as possible to get to Sasha's car. Sasha looked up at me with her reading glasses and bible in hand. "Please take me back to the office." I wipe the tears from my cheeks. Sasha shook her head. "Let's pray, Melinda."

Lord Jesus, I come to you to ask you to bless and watch over my friend. Lord, I ask you if any danger is coming to her and her family life; I ask that you defeat what Satan is trying to do to her. Anoint her head to the sole of her feet. Father God, please heal Melinda, and I ask that you help her get back into serving you and not walk away in dismay. Jesus take over her life; let her know if she gives it all to you, Lord, you will make it all the better in Jesus's name; we pray, Amen.

Amen, I said as we drove in silence back to the office.

For the last few hours, I completed everything I could. I quickly left the office before Sheldon could once again get on my damn nerves with apologizing. I decided to take a shortcut home. Luckily, I did. A familiar truck was parked near the side of a small convenience store. In my mind, I'd seen the truck before. As I got a closer look, my mouth dropped. Oh shit, it was Erick's truck, and I parked next to it. I got sick to my stomach.

Okay, Melinda, get ahold of yourself. I jumped out of my car, and soon as I was about to approach the truck, Stacey Washington came out with a bag of groceries in her hand. Puzzled, Stacey didn't see me at first as she was so busy on her phone. But I knew my ears, and what I heard came out of her mouth was Erick's name. Could she be talking to Erick? Was Erick alive after all these years? As I approached her, Stacey looked up and saw me, and her phone crashed onto the pavement.

"Melinda, is that you? Well, hello, hunny, how are you?"

"I know it's not my business, but who were you on the phone with, and why do you have Erick's truck?"

"Girl, this is my truck since Erick couldn't make the payments. So, I took over, and this is mine."

"I heard you on the phone, and you said Erick's name. Is Erick still alive?"

I got closer to Stacey's face wanting an answer.

"Girl, relax Erick is dead, and I was just talking to one

of Erick's relatives. We were discussing what we were going to do."

Kneeling to pick up her phone, Stacey stuttered and said, "In case you you you ddd.... didn't know well, you should always remember the anniversary of Erick is approaching, and his family wants to place flowers on his grave."

"Where is he buried," I asked Stacey.

"His family has a private burial for family purposes only. I can't disclose that. I gotta go Melinda. "

As I held the truck door open, I shouted, "Family, I have his family, his son Erickson. Doesn't he have the right to know where his father is buried and whatever relatives Erick got? He should know!"

"Melinda, please leave me alone. I can't help you let go of my door," the smoke from Erick's truck hit my face as Stacey shut the door and sped away.

Chapter Ten

"THAT BITCH IS LYING ERICK IS ALIVE, AND I KNOW IT," I screamed.

"What are you talking about Melinda?"

Confused, Pamela was standing in the doorway. I had to drive quickly to Pamela's condo.

"Relax, Melinda, have a seat, and start from the beginning. Let me get you a glass of wine."

I explained everything about what happened and what had been said during my run-in with Stacey.

"Well, did you get the license plate number? I have a friend that can look it up to find out where the truck is registered."

"Damn it, Pamela, No, I didn't."

"Melinda, you were a lawyer; come on, get yourself together. All these clues and evidence are right in your face, and you didn't catch on. Melinda, besides your father, you are also a great lawyer."

"I know, Pamela, I'm just spooked about all this. I served five years, Pamela, you know how rough that was, and to be pregnant, I couldn't raise my son."

"Melinda, I know it's been hard for you, but you are home with your family and friends. We are going to get through this. I promise you we will find the answers. I will call some more favors and see if someone knows about the Erick family's private burial. Let us look at everything that the Tyson family owns, okay."

Pamela kissed me softly on my cheek, making her way to my lips. We kissed passionately. Pamela almost made her way down to my knee-cut dress to lift it above my stomach to get to my pussy. Stiffness and pain from the arousal reminded me that nobody could get a piece of me. I had to, for the first time, tell Pamela not today. Confused and wondering why? I told her I wasn't in the mood as I got up to head home.

***

"So, you made a fool out of me," said my mother. "Who did you pay to send you these?" She pointed to the kitchen countertop.

A huge bouquet of yellow and pink roses was on the counter. "Mother, I don't know who sent me these. Did the person leave a card?" I asked as the missing pic was still between the roses.

"Oh yeah, who is this Sheldon dude, and when are you inviting him over for dinner?"

"So, you're reading my things now."

"Listen Melinda, this is my house," my mother shouted.

"I can read whatever I damn want, and well please." My mother stormed off to her room.
I took the flowers and vase and threw them into the trash can.

"Mommy, are you home," shouted Erickson from upstairs.

"Yes, baby, I'm coming up." My little boy greeted me with a hug and kiss. I couldn't help but hold him a little tighter. Repeatedly Erickson reminded me I was squeezing him too hard. I just couldn't let him go, thinking about what Miss Cleo had told me. I hugged him tight a little bit longer. After placing Erickson in bed, Sheldon blew up my phone, so I answered.

"Hey Melinda, did you like the flowers?"

"Sheldon, you didn't have to get me any flowers."

"But I want to, Melinda. I am, really, I am sorry."

I sighed and resigned. "I accept your apology Sheldon, but we can't do this anymore."

"So, it's someone else," said Sheldon.

"No, it's not anybody else, Sheldon, but I have to go. It's getting late."

***

"You didn't tell that bitch anything, did you?"

Erick's hand gripped tighter around Stacey's neck. Stacey shook her head. No. Coughing heavily to catch her breath. Stacey sat down and explained everything.

"I told your stupid ass to be careful. If Melinda finds out that I'm still alive, it will ruin all my plans. So, if you see her ass again, use this," Erick handed Stacey a gun.

"You know I hate using a gun," said Stacey.

'Well, you better love it now bitch, or that same gun will be in your head just like it was in Kitty's head, do you hear me? Now come over here and get this dick hard."

Erick's dick wasn't the same. It took medication and a lot of work to get the pleasure she remembered from Erick. The bullet gazed at Erick's dick enough for him not to perform normally before the incident. As Erick's stiff dick started to rise up, Erick bent Stacey over on the glass table and pounded her pussy with as much force as he could possibly give her. Finally, after six long hard strokes, Erick's warm nut oozed out of Stacey's pussy onto her thighs.

"Damn it," Erick shouted. "My dick used to kill the pussy having all the bitches who wanted this dick begging for more."

He lit a cigarette puffing heavily. "I'm going to get that bitch where it hurts. Melinda is going to fucking pay. Stacey, call up Travis and have him meet us at the spot. It's time to get one body today."

***

My father Maxwell was in a hurry as he ate breakfast quickly and rushed to explain the details that he was going for a round of golf with a few old high school buddies. Seeing the excitement on my father's face, I was glad he was enjoying his retirement. He pushed everything aside after I had Erickson and raised him while I was in prison. It was time that he gained his freedom and enjoyed himself. Ernest Watson, Frank Douglas, and Ralph Spencer were my dad's best friends through high school. They all gathered together on the golf field with spirits and had a good time reminiscing about the golden days. After a few games and empty beer bottles, the men said their goodbyes and agreed to meet again.

Once my father made it into his car to head home. Out of nowhere, his vehicle started acting strange. Something was wrong. My father tried to slam on the brakes, but they weren't working correctly. As scared as my father was, he tried his best to stop his car safely. As my father swirled into the other lane, he accidentally hit a large truck. Unfortunately, the driver of that truck was injured pretty severely. As for my father, the only thing left to stop his car from hitting another vehicle was to crash into an oak tree.

A witness driving behind my father pulled over to call for help. When help arrived, my father was barely breathing.

A phone call came from my mother's phone as she stormed into my room while I came out of the shower.

MELINDA, YOUR FATHER HAS BEEN IN AN ACCIDENT. BRING YOUR ASS ON; WE GOT TO GO TO THE HOSPITAL.

I threw on something and wrapped my hair in a bun. I called Pamela to come to the hospital and pick up Erickson from school. Pacing back and forth, I didn't know what to suspect as nurses and doctors ran in and out the double doors. I went to the front desk again, and the nurse had to calm me down and inform me that my father was still in surgery.

"Sit your ass down, Melinda. We will know something soon," said my mother. Biting on my nails, I sat down. Finally, the doctor came out and sat my mother and me down to explain the procedure.

"He is stable, but he did lose a lot of blood. Some surgeries still need to be done, but I got the most important one first. I will let you all see him, but only briefly." I saw my father's body lying there with tubes in his mouth and cords all on his body. I broke down and cried; my mother had to calm me down as she massaged my father's head and kissed him on his bruised cheek. I walked over and kissed him on the other cheek. I told my father that I loved him and he would be okay. The night nurse came in and told us visiting hours were over. My mother and I kissed my father one last time. We didn't realize that it was going to be our last goodbye.

Early that morning, I woke up hearing glass crashing as I went downstairs; I saw my mother throwing every piece of crystal glass and plate she could get her hands on and crying heavily. "Mother, what are you doing," I shouted.

"HE GONE, MELINDA. YOUR FATHER IS GONE."

I felt like my heart was about to pop out of my chest. My father can't be dead; he is a fighter, damn it, he is

Maxwell Stone. He couldn't just leave us like this. I was too scared, but I had to comfort my mother. I was surprised for the first time ever; she embraced me and hugged me as we cried together on the kitchen floor.

My father's memorial service was beautiful. People from everywhere who knew my father came to pay their respect, even some of his old clients who my father won their cases came to pay their respect. From afar, where nobody could see, Erick, Stacey, and Travis stood watching and laughing while my father was laid to rest. They watched as loved ones cried and voiced why him lord! The three 'chaos' who committed the crime were drinking and clinging bottles.

"Man Erick," said Travis, "you hit Melinda where it hurts, cutting old pop's brake line as you did."

"It was your idea, cousin," Erick looked at Travis.

"Who the man," said Erick as he chugged a mouth full of beer down his throat.

"You the man-baby," said Stacey as she kissed him passionately. "One down, two more to go," said Erick.

***

"If you need anything, Melinda, don't hesitate to let us know," said Sasha.

All three of my girls embraced me; as my mother walked toward the limo. She passed us and turned around to inform me that everyone would be heading back to the house for refreshments. As I wiped the tears from my eyes, I nodded and got inside the limo.

***

Travis went back with Erick and Stacey to their lay-low place to continue their celebration. Erick threw Travis a roll of money for his service in helping him destroy my father's vehicle. "Ah, cuz," said Travis.

"I'm glad you came back on fucking board with this shit, man. These Stone mutha-fuckers gonna learn not to fuck with our family," Erick said as Stacey returned with more bottles of beer. Handing both men a bottle, Erick, out of nowhere, told Stacey to go up to the room with Travis to give him the time of his life. A confused Stacey looked at Erick and said, "Baby, are you serious? I can't; you promised me this would not happen anymore."

"Bitch do what the fuck I say."

"But I'm your wife." Without saying another word before she felt the sting of Erick's fist hit her cheek, she escorted Travis to the bedroom. Travis, please, let's act like we fucking. I can't do this."

"Bitch please, I need some pussy. I will not dare pass on the free pussy that my cousin is giving up. So, just get on your damn knees and let me shove this dick down your throat."

As Stacey wished Travis had a change of heart, she knew he wouldn't change his mind. Travis slapped Stacey on her face softly to instruct her to open her mouth wide as his dick went deep in Stacey's mouth and down her throat. Stacey was a pro on deep throating any size any type of dick. In her teenage years, she would out beat any bitch who thought they could out beat her on sucking dick, so having a gag reflex was out the window. As saliva dripped from her mouth onto Travis's dick, the pre-cum of Travis shot into the back of her throat as she swallowed the salty flavor of nut down her throat. "Well, aren't you going to return the favor," said Stacey. Travis looked at Stacey, laughed, and informed her that he didn't eat pussy. Travis pushed Stacey onto the bed and inserted his dick inside Stacey's warm wet pussy without considering protection. Travis went deep inside Stacey's walls. She couldn't help to enjoy it since Erick wasn't much of a king in the bedroom; she enjoyed his cousin. Harder and harder, Travis fucked Stacey's pussy deep as she was on all fours. Travis took his large plump thumb and whammed into Stacey's ass. Stacey was having the time of her life grinding her fat ass on Travis's dick while he fucked her ass with his thumb.

"Damn Travis, you got some good dick," Stacey said between moans, which began to get louder and louder. While both were enjoying one another in the bedroom, Travis and Stacey didn't know; Erick watched downstairs. Neither of them knew about the hidden cameras Erick had placed in areas where they laid their heads. Erick continued to watch, furious and jealous about what he heard coming out of Stacey's mouth. Travis pounded Stacey's pussy so good she climaxed to a peak that the inside of her pussy was throbbing like a beat of a drum.

Then, without giving her a warning, Travis shoved his large thick dick inside Stacey's ass and anally fucked her like there was no tomorrow. With each deep stroke, Travis slapped Stacey's round ass, and each sting gave Stacey a rush to let Travis know this was some good ass he couldn't pass up and will be coming back for more.

Pound after pound, Stacey's ass began to open. She steadied herself to continue getting fucked from behind. Finally, Travis let out a loud moan, and his warm nut shot inside Stacey's ass. One last slap on the ass for a big thank you, Travis put his pants on and walked out the room.

"Enjoy yourself, cuz (cousin)," Erick said as he poured himself a glass of Henny.

"Damn, cuz I see why you married her," chuckled Travis.

"Naw, it's not like that-that bitch been down with me from day one with many fucked up shit I've done. But she still rode with me. Care for a shot," said Erick as he refilled his cup.

"Naw, I gotta bounce cuz, hit me up on the next gig," said Travis.

Immediately after Travis left, Erick went upstairs to see tired Stacey on her stomach, fast asleep. As Erick looked down, he could see Travis's nut all inside his girl. His cousin's cum sat all sticky and almost dry between her ass cheeks. Mad Erick turned Stacey around on her back, and blow after blow smacked Stacey across her face as Stacey screamed for Erick to stop. Finally, he repeated what she told Travis and asked, "Oh, so that nigga dick better than mine bitch?"

With a bloody lip and possibly a broken nose, Erick's punches kept coming. After hitting Stacey multiple times across her face, Stacey got up with tears in her eyes and was confused. How did Erick know what she told Travis? With blood coming from her nose and lips,

Stacey yelled, "I didn't want to do this shit; you told me this would not happen anymore. The last time I did this was with your brother Silk and Kitty, and you promised that would be the last time I would be shared with any niggas. You lied to me, Erick," and she stormed into the bathroom to clean herself up. Erick stood up, shouted fuck you bitch, and walked out of the room.

***

Since my father's passing, the house has been quiet. My mother was locked up in the master bedroom she and my father once shared. I passed by my father's study room, wishing he would be sitting next to his desk if I opened the door. Pamela approved my leave from work with as much time I felt was needed to mourn my father's death. Going back to work wasn't a place to be at the moment. My father's right-hand man, Joe Franklin, came over to read the final testament of my father's will. My father left the house to my mother; he also stated that I could live in the home as long as I wanted. He would continue to pay Devin's hospital bills and medication for as long as Devin is living. My father even left a significant amount for Erickson once he turned eighteen and finished two years in college to get the lump sum of money he left behind.

***

Daydreaming about my father and missing his warm presence around the house, I got distracted by a call on my cell. I looked at the number Otis Peterson. This is not a good time to talk, Otis, I rudely shouted before saying hello. "Melinda, I'm so sorry about your father, Mr. Maxwell's death, but I have to see you. We must meet. Can I please stop by immediately?"

While my mother hadn't been out of the room in days, I instructed Otis to come over. Otis came right on time. I opened the door and instructed him to sit in the dining room. He held an envelope in his arm while taking off his hat and coat.

"So, what is this big news you need to tell me?" I asked as I sat across from him in my father's favorite chair.

"Mr. Peterson, you need to make your point quick before...," I was interrupted as my mother entered the dining area.

"Melinda, who was at the door," my mother came out of my father's bedroom. "What the hell are you doing here? I'm calling the police," shouted my mother.

"Get the fuck out of my house! You think you can just come up here and rekindle a relationship with my daughter that you disowned for years!"

As I was trying to calm my mother down and telling her to relax, in my heart, I wanted her to repeat that I was her daughter.

"Mother, Mr. Peterson came over because he had something very important to tell me. Why don't you go lay down and rest, and I'll make you some tea."

"NO, I want to hear what this ass hole has to say." My mother sat down in my father's chair.

"Please, Mr. Otis, I hope this is something major you wanted to tell me."

Otis sat back down, opened the envelope, and said, "I pulled a couple of strings to get this information, Melinda. Your father, the man that raised you in my absence. His death wasn't an accident. It was murder."

"What do you mean his death wasn't an accident. A car came and hit him out of nowhere, and he died," said my mother. Otis pulled out another piece of paper. "In the police report, they left out one thing Martha," he showed her the paper and another one attached to it. "Your father's brake lines were cut."

"WHAT," I said.

"Mommy, what's wrong," as Erickson came down the stairs.

"Baby, go back to your room and play with your toys. Mommy will be up in a minute to run your bath."

They waited until Erickson was out of earshot, and Otis continued talking.

"Melinda, this could be you know who that killed Maxwell."

Confused, my mother asked, "What do you mean 'you know who?"

"Mother, this will sound strange, but you remember his daughter Victoria Peterson aka Kitty."

"Yes, I do; why?"

"Well, her death wasn't an accident. We both believe that

Erick is responsible for her death and daddy's as well."

"That's insane Erick is dead; you went to prison for that situation."

"Yes, I did go to prison, but have you seen his body? Was there a funeral of some sort?"

"I don't know, Melinda," stated my mother as my mother got up and escorted herself back to the room.

"Otis, see yourself out, please." Otis got his belongings and walked to the door.

He turned and looked at me. "Melinda, I know I'm not crazy. I know Erick is still alive; be careful and keep your family safe. This man is dangerous, but you should already know that."

I walked Otis to his car and watched him drive away; then, I checked the mailbox for mail. Walking back inside the house and shifting through the mail, I noticed a surprise, another letter from Money.

> *Hey boo,*
> *I've been thinking about you so much I can't get you off my mind. I'm not going to express myself to you about you. You already know how I feel about your sexy ass. I heard about your father on the news, and the girls and I want to give our condolences to you and your family. Stay strong, my love. I hope to share this good news with you- that will put a smile on your face. In a few months, I will be coming home. I got approved, and we can finally be together, baby. I hope you are happy and I hope I put a smile on your lovely face. Well, I'm cutting this letter short, stay*

*strong, and once we meet again, I want to make
love to you like old times.... Take care.*

Love, Money

Finally, good news has been brought to my attention. Money is coming home. I went upstairs to check up on Erickson; he finally went to sleep after his bath and story time. I prepared a hot shower and positioned myself and my adjustable shower head the same way I did in Costa Rica. Instead of thinking about Erick between my legs, I thought about Money as I climaxed and let the hot water trickle down my legs. Early Wednesday morning, I was surprised that my mother agreed to watch Erickson while I went back to the law firm to work. Everyone greeted me sweetly even though I hadn't been in the office for over a month. A portrait of my father was on the wall with a small engraved writing underneath that said Beloved father, beloved lawyer, and beloved friend. Rest in peace, Maxwell Stone.

I thanked everyone for attending the funeral and for their love, support, hard work, and dedication to my father. Then, I instructed everyone to get back to work. "Well, well, I see someone back and ready to work." I turned only to see Sheldon Mitchell standing by my desk. "Hello Sheldon, how are you?"

"You have been avoiding me, Melinda. I understand you needed time, but I can't help but think about you. I need you again; let's meet up tonight. I want to feel your wet juices all over my dick."

"Sheldon, we're at work, and you fucked up my pussy. I was sore for weeks!" I explained and stated we couldn't anymore. He pleaded like a baby.

"I didn't mean to hurt you, Melinda. This time I will be gentle, and when you want me to stop, I will do so," he placed his right hand where his heart was in his chest. I believe he meant every word. After that, I eventually agreed to meet Sheldon back at his place, but right after, he and I met Pamela in the conference room to discuss what Otis Peterson had told me.

Everyone had left, and the three of us gathered at the conference table, and I explained the new piece of news. I hoped that Pamela and Sheldon didn't think I was crazy when I told them I still believed Erick was alive.

"We got to find this son of a bitch," said Pamela. "You look a hot mess and very stressed, Melinda. This shit is bothering you badly. Have you gone back to talk to the therapist?"

"No, I didn't think about going back." I was feeling the atmosphere in the room. I looked at Pamela, and her expression with everything I had stated.

"Look, at this point, even if nobody believes me, I know Erick is out there somewhere, and I will prove it to you, my mother, and everybody else that doesn't believe me."

I really thought Pamela would have my back and believe every word I said and that I wasn't crazy. I stormed out of the office, drove to Sheldon as promised, and waited. He came home, and before saying anything, I kissed Sheldon, pushed him into his apartment, and fucked his brains out.

***

I needed to get away for a while to clear my head, and I decided to go on a getaway with just Erickson. So, I booked a flight for Miami to rest and relax on the beautiful beach. Once there, we settled down into our hotel and ordered room service. Erickson was sound asleep when I gathered all the paperwork handed to me by Otis. I sat and prepared my investigation on the whereabouts of Erick's location. The detailed evidence on each paper had me suspicious. "I need to get a copy of Stacey's phone records," I murmured. I looked at the clock, and it was almost midnight. I gathered all the papers, placed them back into a folder, and snuggled next to my son.

The next day Erickson and I sat and played in the sand on the beach. As the warm sun hit my smooth caramel skin, I watched Erickson build his first sandcastle. People were having a good time enjoying the warm breeze and the ocean at the beach. Then, out of nowhere, a tall, muscular man came walking toward me as he left the ocean. His body was drenched in water. "Damn, he's fine," I said.

"Mommy, that's a bad word."

"Sorry, baby," I said to Erickson.

As the man came my way, I could have sworn I had seen him before. He looked so familiar. I had never approached men before, but I had to know his name. I got up from my beach towel and stopped him from walking past me.

"Excuse me, but don't I know you from somewhere? You look so familiar?"

The man looked me up and down and licked his bottom lip before speaking. "Is that your way of introducing yourself," he chuckled.

"Oh no, sorry, I just thought I'd seen you from somewhere. If I am wrong, then I'm sorry. My name is Melinda Stone," and I extended my hand to him. A grin came upon his face.

"We have met before, Ms. Stone. My name is Travis Freeman. We met on a trip to Costa Rica. I was with my frat brothers Sheldon Mitchell, Jamal Taylor, and Frankie Scott."

"Oh yeah, I remember. I knew you looked familiar. How have you been?"

As Travis and I reunited and chatted a bit, I couldn't help asking myself why I never got the chance to get to know him. Damn, Travis was fine.

"How about we have a couple of drinks if you are available tonight," I asked as I gently touched Travis's wet abs.

"Mommy, I'm hungry," cried Erickson.

"Who is this cute fella," Travis asked.

"Well, this is my son Erickson; say hello, Erickson." Erickson waved hello. Looking at Erikson, are you ready to go back to the hotel?"

I gathered our belongings and waited for Travis's response to my offer. Little did he know I would love to be in his arms right now, but I had to be casual while being on vacation with my son.

"Well, I will have to take a raincheck on that offer, beautiful," Travis said. "But how bout we exchange numbers, and we can hang out some other time."

Travis departed, but he didn't hesitate to call Erick and give him the news about who he saw on the beach. Erick was furious and demanded Travis's return visit to discuss plans to take another out. But, Travis thought, why end the fun? Why waste pussy before killing Melinda? I'm going to get some tonight. Travis agreed to what Erick said, ended the call, and went to the bar.

Travis texted me that he wanted to meet up, and I gave him the hotel and my suite number. I prepared Erickson for his bath and watched a little bit of television. It was almost that time for Travis to come, so I ordered room service and purchased their best bottle of wine. On time with his sleeping routine, Erickson went fast to sleep, and I placed him in the other bedroom and waited for Travis to arrive. Travis came and looked better than he did at the beach. I took in every detail of his body as I waited for him to enter. We chatted and laughed. I didn't know that Travis and I had so much in common. The bottle of wine we shared was empty, and we sat there gazing into each other's eyes. Travis moved my curly hair from my shoulder. He kissed my neck as his warm tongue made circular movements on my collarbone. My silk underwear got utterly soaked. Travis removed my robe, pulled me to the edge of the couch, spread my legs, and sucked on my pussy. My tightened walls opened up, dripping every amount of juice. Travis continued to lick and nibble on my clitoris. I wanted to moan loudly, but I didn't want to wake up Erickson. I lifted Travis's head from my pussy and escorted him to the other room. I pushed Travis onto the bed, enjoying the view of his body.

I noticed the brand-named sweatpants, which showed the imprint of his dick in attention, hard and heavy. I got on my knees and discovered Travis was not wearing underwear. His massive dick was held in the palm of my hands; as I massaged it gently with both hands. The veins in his dick appeared for anybody to see. I licked my lips, opened my mouth as wide as I could, and sucked the head of Travis's dick. I tried to do my best to deep throat, but I couldn't fit a lot down my throat with the gagging reflex and his size. I took as much as I could before coughing. Travis sat there grinding his hips and heavily moaning as he took his hands and placed them around my neck; then, with one hand, he grabbed a handful of my hair and shoved his dick deeper inside my mouth. My jaw began to hurt. I did everything I could to keep sucking his dick. But Travis pulled his dick out of my mouth and instructed me to get on the bed. He flicked his tongue on my hard round nipples and trailed his way down to my navel and then to my pussy. My legs were raised high to the ceiling as Travis continued to suck my pussy. I was ready for Travis to enter me, and I begged him that I wanted his dick. Travis entered me, and it was like heaven. Each long deep stroke and the rhythmic pounding rub against my walls felt so damn good; I couldn't get enough.

I wrapped my legs around Travis's waist. Picking me up from the bed, Travis placed my back on the bedroom door. Travis held onto my ass. While I rode him standing, he bit my neck. Travis and I fucked while standing, which seemed for hours until we changed position, and he kneeled me down on all fours and fucked me from behind. The sting of his hands slapped my ass repeatedly as I continued to bounce and rock my ass up and down on his dick. Travis grabbed another handful of my hair and drew me closer to his chest. He went deeper inside my wet pussy as he pulled my neck back and kissed my lips.

Travis let go of my hair and held my head down on the bed fucking me deeper and deeper. I tried to breathe and gasped for air periodically as my head was buried deep within the thick covers.

Travis took hold of one of my legs and held it on his shoulder. I positioned myself to stay in this position as long as Travis wanted while fucking me harder than ever. The pain from my leg on Travis's shoulder began to hurt me. I tried to move my leg, but Travis slapped my ass and kept pounding. Travis started to remind me of Sheldon as the force of his dick made me sore. Finally, Travis released my leg from his shoulder and laid on the bed. I thought he was finished, but he told me to get on top and ride him. Before riding his thick massive dick, Travis pulled my pussy to his lips and sucked on my swollen lips. The pain hurt yet felt so good. I rode Travis's tongue until he slapped my ass and was ready for me to fuck him. I rode Travis so hard and good. I placed his hands behind his head and kept my balance on my tiptoes. I rode him on the bed. Travis's eyes rolled to the back of his head, feeling the effects of my actions. He repositioned and lifted me; Travis had me ride him backward. I held on to his ankles and rode him the way he instructed me.

While he held on to my ass and rubbed his thumbs on my anal, I was hoping that Travis wouldn't do the same thing Erick did at my condo on my kitchen stool; but before I knew it and said anything, the pain of my ass began to open. Travis placed his dick right inside my ass and began fucking me. I felt every upward and deep thrust into my ass as I held onto his ankles. He bounced my ass up and down on his dick, and I was past ready for Travis to nut. My ass began to open up little by little with each stroke. But the pain was getting worse. After a few more deep strokes and a loud moan, Travis finally came, and I felt the warmth inside my ass. I got up and felt the warmth of the cum oozing out and trickling down my thighs.

"Damn, that was good," Travis said while breathing heavily. I smiled and agreed and exited to the bathroom.

<h1 style="text-align:center">Chapter Eleven</h1>

Our trip came to an end. I packed Erickson and my belongings and called a cab, and we headed to the airport. Our plane landed safely, and when our cab reached our home, Erickson noticed a woman standing by the gate of my parent's home. "Mommy, who is that lady?" He pointed at the woman as the cab came to a stop and parked, and the driver opened our doors to exit the vehicle. I looked at the woman wearing a white t-shirt, faded jeans with socks, slides, and a baseball cap. I noticed her face. It was Money.

"Hey, my love." Money grabbed and hugged me

"Money, what are you doing here?"

"I came to see you, baby. You're not happy to see me," stated Money.

"I am happy, but why didn't you call me to let me know you were coming. Then, I could have arranged for you to meet me somewhere or purchase a room for you."

"With what phone, Melinda damn," said Money.

I paid the cab driver, took Erickson's hand, and walked to the gate.

"Is this the little man," said Money.

"His name is Erickson, and yes, this is my son."

We walked into the house while Money followed behind. My mother was in the kitchen cleaning. Grandma Erickson yelled, running to give her a hug. While holding Erickson in her arms, my mother looked up and asked about Money. I told my mother that Money was a client that needed my service. I asked my mother to fix Erickson a snack and that Money, and I would be in my father's studies to discuss her case. I hope my mother didn't realize I was lying, but I had to help Money.

I helped Money get into a hotel until she got on her feet and told her I would do my best to see her later that night. As I called a cab, I gave Money my cell number and told her to call me once she entered her room. I gave her some cash for food or whatever she wanted.

She left without saying much. Then, a text came through on my phone, and it was Travis, letting me know what a fantastic night he had with me. I text him back with a smiling emoji. Travis texted back, wondering if we could meet up again. As I replied, I would let him know when I'm available.

Looking at everything, I knew I had to see Money, so she didn't get the wrong idea of me not wanting to see her. So, I entered the hotel where Money was staying, and I knocked on the door of her room. Money pulled me inside, closed the door, and started kissing me.

She kissed me so softly, the way she did the first time we made love together in the cell we shared. Money picked me up and carried me to the bed. She took off my shoes and started kissing my ankles, trailing up to my legs until she got to my thighs and kissed both my legs softly. Even though I'm still sore from Travis, I couldn't let Money know. For I knew she still had a jealous attitude. She spread my legs apart and pulled down my panties. When Money kissed my pussy and rubbed my clit, I wanted to jump from the slight pain I felt. But I couldn't let Money notice my reaction. She continued pleasuring me as she spread my lips apart and her thick tongue entered inside.

Once Money and I made passionate love, I slept in Money's arms and went to sleep as she held me close to her. The following day we got breakfast and hung out. I purchased Money, a new wardrobe and shoes. We returned to the hotel, where Money continually wanted more of me. While waiting for a guest to exit the building, Money held onto my waist and sucked on my earlobe. I snickered for her not to do that in public cause little did we know; we were being watched. Across the street, angry with tears in her eyes, Pamela sat in her car watching another woman hold me.

"THAT BITCH LIED TO ME," she screamed and drove off in a rage.

***

At the office, I couldn't get Pamela's attention. She was acting so strange that finally, once alone, I went to my old office and closed the door to find out what was wrong with my friend.

"Please get the fuck out of my office, Melinda. I don't want to talk to you."

"What did I do?" I stated as I was clueless on why Pamela was talking to me that way.

"Are you hard of hearing? Go back to your area, take calls, handle the paperwork and get out of my office."

"I don't know what the fuck is wrong with you, Pamela, but don't take your shit out on me as a friend. I came to check up on you."

As I opened the door to exit, Pamela shouted out, "You lied to me about not having a relationship with another bitch. I saw your trifling ass with that bodybuilder bitch.'"

Fuck Pamela caught me with Money. Pamela instructed me to leave her office again as I turned around to explain. As I walked away from her office, my thoughts were on my actions. I can't believe I let this get so far. I should not have led Pamela on like this. We have been friends for way too long. I just hope she can find it in her heart to forgive me.

Later that evening, after work, I tried again. I wanted to speak with Pamela and for her to hear me out. I knocked on her complex door, but she wouldn't let me inside. People gathered out in the hallway to see what the commotion was about as I explained myself to Pamela's closed door.

I didn't care who heard my truth. People watched, listened, and before I got to my most intimate details about my life with her and the way she and Money made love to my body; before talking about how Money made love to me some nights while pregnant with Erickson, Pamela opened the door forcefully and pulled me inside.

"BITCH, are you trying to put me out of my condo, or worse, let my noisy ass neighbors know about my private life," said Pamela.

"I was going to say whatever to get you to open the door for me to explain, and it worked," I said.

"Why did you lie to me? If you would have kept it one hundred, told me the truth, then I wouldn't act this way towards you, Melinda. I have fucking feelings too," cried Pamela.

"Knowing that another woman is making love to my girl would hurt me, but at least you would have been honest with me."

"I didn't mean to hurt you, Pammie. Please forgive me; I'm sorry." I wiped the tears from her eyes.

"What else are you hiding that you are not telling me, Melinda?"

I didn't want to tell Pamela I slept with Sheldon, but she was waiting to see if I had any more secrets, so I told her the truth. Her mouth opened wide.

"WHAT THE FUCK, MELINDA! You fucked Sheldon?"

I explained everything in detail and told her everything, even how Tasha knew and took me to the hospital;

devastated and pissed off, Pamela listened to me explain. Then, letting her curiosity get the best of her, Pamela asked, "Was he good, and did he have a big one?"

I laughed and told her hell yeah. Pamela nodded and smiled. "I figured his dick was, as he wore those nice suits. I've wanted a piece of his ass since I hired him. But at least somebody got a piece of him. We both laughed.

"Glad you forgave me, Pamela," and I kissed her.

"Prove to me how sorry you are, Melinda."

Pamela got off the stool and let her robe fall to the floor. Then, she sat on top of her countertop and opened her legs. I smiled, walked over to Pamela, and began tasting her. I held onto Pamela's thighs, and placed them both on my shoulders. Then, I went to work with my tongue. Pamela's head hung back as she held tight to the countertop. As her soft moan turned me on, I continued sucking every drop of her. Pamela gently rubbed her clit with the tip of her fingertips and sucked each tip, tasting her sweetness off her hands. Melinda, I'm bout to cum, baby; keep sucking my pussy Pamela screamed as she held onto my ponytail.

I made sucking noises on Pamela's pussy, making her coo like a baby. Finally, Pamela's intense orgasm released, and her juices trickled between my lips. A knock at Pamela's door startled us. Without thinking that Pamela was naked on the countertop and her scent was on my lips, I opened the door, and there stood Sheldon with folders to give Pamela.

"Hey, Melinda, what brings you by."

Sheldon entered without being greeted to come in. Then, glancing around, he noticed Pamela. He looked at us both and asked me directly.

"What's going on here, Melinda?"

As Pamela jumped off the countertop and grabbed her robe off the floor, I explained.

"Sheldon, it's not what you think."

Pointing at the both of us, "So you and Melinda sleeping together? How long has this been going on? I want some answers."

We spent some time explaining to Sheldon how we had this fling since college. We thought we were over it until I came home from prison and how it just sort of restarted, and we have been sleeping together ever since. Sheldon looked at us with a questioning look on his face.

"Sheldon, please don't let this get out; please, I'll do anything," I said.

Sheldon nodded in agreement as he placed the folders on the counter, then walked over to me and asked, "Anything?" as his hand caressed my face, and his lips touched mine and kissed me.

He tasted Pamela on my lips, knowing the situation and obviously, not caring. His tongue danced inside my mouth, exploring me, and I kissed him passionately. He turned to me as he accepted the situation, and I took his cue that he wanted in on the action. I unzipped his pants and pulled out his dick. I was caressing him with long strokes when Pamela came over and removed my hand, and her lips went to work sucking on Sheldon's dick. Sheldon became mindless of thought; as he took pleasure in the night that started with him bringing folders to Pamela's place.

As I was watching the interaction. My pussy got wet thinking of all that was about to take place, and I fantasized about the pleasure Pamela would receive, knowing the feeling of being fucked by Sheldon Mitchell.

We entered Pamela's bedroom. Pamela continued to pleasure Sheldon while Sheldon sucked on my hardened nipples. Then he instructed me to straddle his face. I wanted to tell Sheldon I was fine, but he insisted I do what I was told. As I climbed onto his face, Sheldon's tongue circled my pussy, and his head game was finally on point. It wasn't the best, but it was better than last. Pamela couldn't wait much longer. She reached for a condom from her nightstand, placed it on Sheldon's dick, and rode him. Pamela managed to affirm what I told her earlier.

"Melindaaaa, you are not lying," she said between thrusts, "Sheldon does have a big dick. OMG!"

I moved away and watched Pamela ride Sheldon as he grabbed Pamela's waist and fucked her pussy. Then Sheldon rolled Pamela over and fucked her from behind as Pamela cooed him to go deeper and harder. She pointed to me while I was sitting in a chair to come over to her. Pamela opened my legs and paid attention to eating my pussy while Sheldon fucked her from behind. Sheldon pulled out, took off the condom, came over to me, and had me suck his dick. The nasty flavor from the condom entered my mouth, and I sucked Sheldon's dick as Pamela had her way, feasting on my pussy.

The three of us laid tired and naked on Pamela's cotton sheets as Sheldon breathed heavily, looking at Pamela and me stretched out on the bed. After a moment, Sheldon pulled Pamela towards him and spoke round two starts now as he dove his head between Pamela's legs. I watched Pamela bite her bottom lip and enjoy the pleasure Sheldon gave. I couldn't help but think that my girl finally got what she'd been craving. Sheldon put on another condom, wrapped Pamela's legs around him, and pounded her pussy as she dug her manicured nails into Sheldon's chest. Sheldon instructed me to bend over, informing me that it was my turn after Pamela.

I kneeled, waiting for him to hit it from behind. Pamela played with my nipples with her tongue as she placed her hand under my pussy to get me ready for Sheldon. Sheldon moved over as my ass was up in the air and ready. He inserted his massive dick in my pussy, and I moaned. Sheldon went to work fucking me from behind. Pamela came over and rubbed my back, telling me to take all that dick while spreading and smacking my ass. As she kept cheering me on, I bounced my ass while Sheldon continued to pound my insides to a pulp. Before I knew it, Sheldon told Pamela and me to lay down as our heads hung on the end of the mattress, and our mouths opened wide; he loaded both our mouths with his nut. Before Pamela could even swallow, Sheldon shoved his dick down her throat. He rode her face as he released the heightened arousal precum. Her eyes got wider with tears, and her saliva dripped down the side of her face. Sheldon pulled his dick out of Pamela's mouth, and precum oozed out the head of his penis. He came over to me, and I licked the remainder of his precum off. While he held his dick, Sheldon gave a deep throaty sound and shot his release on my face. After calming down, Sheldon patted my swollen pussy and Pamela's mouth and said, "That was amazing. Ya'll secret safe with me."

Checking my phone, I noticed I had a lot of missed calls from Money. *Damn!* There's no way I could see her now, especially after what just happened at Pamela's place. I decided to talk to her later and headed home to Erickson. Luckily my mother was sound asleep still in my father's master bedroom and didn't hear me come in. I walked upstairs to run a hot bath, but when I entered my room, I was greeted by Money. I closed the door and was surprised at how the hell she got in my room, let alone how she got in the gate. I forgot that Money was a mastermind. She could break or hack into anything.

"You shouldn't be here, Money if my mother finds you..."

"Relax, baby; I just wanted to see you. Come here, and give me a kiss."

I pushed Money away and instructed her to leave. I couldn't kiss Money or look into her eyes after I had just done.

"You smell like you been fucking someone anyway," Money said.

"I thought you told me you'd wait for me, Melinda. I thought you loved and wanted to be with me."

Money got so angry and loud with her conversation that I swore she would wake up my mother. "Money, I'm sorry; I never meant to hurt you. I do care about you. It's just that I have so much that I'm dealing with right now."

Money opened the door to my balcony and lit a cigarette as she looked at my guilty body. I hope that mother fucker was worth it. As she reached into her pocket, pulled out a small box, and threw it at my feet, "I thought you were special, Melinda."

Money climbed to the end of the balcony, safely let herself down to the ground, lifted the broken gate board that my father had forgotten to fix years ago, and exited out. I opened the box that Money had thrown at me, and to my surprise, it was a 10k princess cut with a channel set accent. On the inside read, Money and Melinda forever.

***

The following day, I went downstairs to see what my mother had prepared Erickson and me for breakfast. There wasn't an aroma of cooking in the air, and the kitchen was clean. My mom wrote a note on the counter. She had gone out for a while and would be home later. I was glad she was getting some fresh air and was out. I knew she loved my father, and with his passing, she knew they wouldn't grow old together, which devastated her. Being married for 15 years before my mother cheated, no other man could treat her like my father Maxwell did. Erickson came downstairs. I prepared him some cereal and got his clothes ready for school. Once I dropped my son off, I headed to the office. It was a massive relief that we kept our private business behind closed doors, for none of the staff suspected anything. Sheldon and Pamela greeted each other and went on with their everyday routine. The day rushed by quickly; I got Erickson from school and went home. It was almost five pm with no sign of my mother returning home. This was strange, but I didn't pay it any mind.

My mother was grown and what she does is her business. I ordered Chinese food for Erickson, and we watched a movie until we passed out on the oversized couch. The following day arrived, and there was still no sign of my mother returning home. I never knew or remembered if my mother had any female or male friends. So, I didn't know who to call to find her whereabouts. I went about my regular duties. I dropped off Erickson at school and went to work. I dialed my mother's phone number with every available opportunity but still got her voicemail.

"Is everything okay?" Mr. Chester, the janitor who was pushing his cart of supplies, asked.

"I'm okay, Mr. Chester; how are you?"

As we chit-chatted till the phone rang, I politely waved goodbye and answered the phone. After work and getting Erickson again from school, still no sign of my mother returning home. I did what most people would do, I dialed 911 and filed a missing person report. Two officers arrived at my door. I informed them that I hadn't seen my mother. I showed them the note that she had placed on the counter. I gave them her cell number, and with the little information to go by, the officers left to investigate locating my mother.

I wanted to stay positive, so I kept reminding myself that my mother was okay. She probably went on another me, myself, and I cruise, and she would be home soon. I prepared myself each day as I continued living daily with Erickson taking him back and forth to school and heading to work. My stomach was upsetting me as negative thoughts ran across my mind. *Get it together, Melinda; your mother is fine; the police will find her and bring her home. Everything will be okay,* I said to myself. Another two days had gone by, and still, no sign of my mother returning home.

I called several times to speak with both officers that came to the house. They informed me repeatedly that they were working on finding my mother and would keep me posted on what they found. A week had passed, and I thought that something had to be wrong. So, I located my keys for Erickson and me to hang out at the park. The two officers I spoke with approached the gate and drove up into the driveway. Officer Johnson and officer Franklin greeted me and asked if they could speak with me for a second. I instructed Erickson to go up to his room as he sadly repeated to me, "But mommy, I thought we were going to the park?"

"We will, baby; let me speak to these nice officers, and once they leave, we will go okay, baby."

Nodding his little head, Erickson went upstairs. I kindly asked the two gentlemen to come inside and offer to prepare a hot cup of coffee, and both declined and sat down.

"Ms. Stone, we came here today to inform you about some critical information we've found. But, before telling you this," said Officer Johnson, "We don't know for sure until we run some tests and get back to you with the results."

Eager for them to come out and say what they found, I shouted, "What is it? Have you found my mother?"

"No, ma'am," said officer Franklin, "We located her car an hour and a half away from your home. Inside the vehicle on the driver's side was a large amount of blood."

"WHAT!" I screamed, "No, NO, NO! Please tell me that you are joking," I said. "Please tell me this can't be real."

"Ms. Stone, we don't know if your mother's blood is in that seat. We'd like you to come by the station when you have time for our lab staff to draw blood and run some tests. We want to see if the blood inside your mother's car is hers," said Officer Franklin.

"Her car is under investigation, as we are looking for any evidence left behind. Please trust us; we will find your mother," said Officer Johnson.

Both officers excused themselves and walked out the door. When the door clicked shut, I grabbed my cell and called everyone I could think of to come to the house. Pamela, Tasha, Sasha, Sheldon, and believe it or not, Otis Peterson came over to figure out what was going on and why I was shaken up.

****

All eyes were on me as they sat, and some stood in my home. I began to get them up to date about my mother.

"It has been a week since I hadn't heard or spoke with my mother. So, I decided to file a missing person report. Two officers handling my mother's case just left and told me they had located my mother's vehicle and that a massive amount of blood was inside her car. But they don't know whether it is hers. So, I have to go to the station to test my blood or DNA. I forget."

I said everything as my tears got heavier and fell rapidly from my eyes. Every one of my friends gathered around to calm me down. Otis instantly spoke out and said, "This is Erick's doing, Melinda, and he is too damn smart to leave any trace of himself behind."

"I really don't know if this is Erick doing this shit Otis; all I know is I can't lose another parent."

Pamela rubbed my shoulder as I cried in her arms. Sheldon got up and paced back and forth around the room.

"I wonder if this guy Erick has someone working for him, as his right-hand man. You said his brother Silk had a partner he trusted that he thought would never fuck him over. What's his name?" Sheldon snapped his finger to remember who Silk's right-hand man was.

I blurted out, "Sammie Watson."

"Yeah, Sammie Watson. What if Erick has the same someone who isn't like Sammie but has Erick's back." All of us in the living room agreed with Sheldon's statement.

"I never met any of Erick's male friends. I only saw one particular person: the girl I accidentally shot, who fucked Erick in my condo, Stacey Washington."

"Did you say Stacey Washington," asked Otis?

"Yes, why do you know her?"

"I heard of her," said Otis. "I believe she's accountable for Victoria's death as well."

"Let's just say a prayer," said Sasha. "So, everyone, let's gather around while I pray to our heavenly father."

Everyone joined hands, and as Sasha was about to pray, Tasha ghetto ass interrupted her and shouted to Sasha... "Mrs. Sasha Morgan, wassup with your belly?" Sasha smiled and answered Tasha. "We will speak about that another time. We are here for Melinda now."

I knew Tasha wasn't going to let that go. So, I looked at Sasha. "Go ahead and tell them," I said. "We will at least be hearing some good news today."

Sasha cleared her throat and told everyone in the living room that she was expecting. Everyone congratulated her, and she gave everyone a big thank you. Then Sasha redirected everyone back to the task of praying, and it was a heartfelt prayer that was needed.

I was glad that Sasha offered to take Erickson to her house while I headed to the station for someone to run my DNA on the blood found inside my mother's car. Thankfully Otis insisted that he stay over and take me to the police station. Mother would have been pissed if she found out that I let Otis spend the night. She would have been even more pissed that I let him use the guest room that was her room after she and my father Maxwell filed for divorce.

Early in the following morning, Otis and I got up and headed to the station. One of the laboratory staff took my blood and informed me when I would hear the results. Otis waited for me in the waiting room. He embraced me with a hug for the first time, doing what was needed for a daughter who had lost her father's love. As the tears kept coming that day, I forgave Otis for not being in my life all those years. Because right now, at this most critical point in my life, I needed Otis the most. We sat at a coffee shop to discuss everything, as Sheldon's idea kept running through my head that Erick may have someone helping him. But who and have I ever come across the guy? Still confused and lost at the same time. I ate a peaceful lunch with Otis and asked him to take me home to be alone and rest.

After what seemed like forever, the results came back from the lab. I got an unsuspected call that I didn't want to hear. It felt like my heart jumped right out of my chest. The blood from the car was indeed my mother's, but her body was still not found. My silent cries began.

" I lost both of my parents. Who would want my parents dead? Neither had enemies; both were well-loved."

While I didn't want company over, I texted everyone the horrible news. Everyone wanted to come over to see if I was okay; I declined. The house was too quiet. I wasn't used to not hearing my mother's voice, the sound of the way she yelled at me. I thought about how we didn't have a great relationship, but I still loved her deep down. A couple of months passed by, and finally, my mother's body was found by some hikers hiking in the woods. They discovered my mother's lifeless body in a ditch. I didn't want to believe that my mother was dead. I felt so sick to my stomach as I screamed in pain and rage.

"Mommy, what's wrong?" Erickson asked as he walked into my room. I had to explain that Grandma is now with grandpa Maxwell. Confused, Erickson asked, "Mommy, who hurt grandma?"

"I don't know, baby. I don't know," as I kissed his little cheeks and held him close to me.

Chapter Eleven

I looked through the clear glass as the examiner uncovered my mother's body. I nodded my head. It was indeed my mother. She was severely cut; I counted at least five cuts on her body. Officer Johnson and Officer Franklin escorted me to another room and discussed everything. We are so sorry about your loss Ms. Stone," said Officer Franklin; he cleared his throat and said, "Your mother suffered from multiple stab wounds. The examiner counted at least ten open wounds located on her body. What killed her was the wound inflicted in her abdominal area, where she lost a lot of blood. We found traces of blood inside the trunk of her car that also matched your mother's. She had been inside the trunk when she took her last breath, and then the killer abandoned her body in the woods. Although we did not recover her purse or cell phone, which we believe the killer kept, we will get to the bottom of this. We will solve this case and find out who killed your mother." I got up and thanked the two officers.

Retrieving my phone from my purse, I noticed a missed call from a non-familiar number highlighted on the front screen. I unlock my phone and listen to the voicemail. I wasn't ready for what I was about to hear.

Hello, this is Debbie Clark. I'm one of the nurses here at the Strong Faith Hope facility. I'm trying to reach Ms. Melinda Stone. Please get in touch with me as soon as possible.

I relistened to the message and called the facility. *I was not ready for what I was about to hear.* I redialed the number and spoke with Debbie.

"Ms. Stone, I hate to inform you that your brother Devin Stone committed suicide this morning," I sat down in the police station lobby as Ms. Clark continued to talk. "I'm so sorry for your loss. If there is anything that the staff can do, please let us know." During our conversation, Debbie gave me information about the day of my mother's disappearance while giving me information about Devin. She told me that my brother had done well taking his medication and attending his therapy sessions and appointments. He was getting the best treatment even though, at times, he was clueless about who people were; she informed me with all that he was a great client.

Debbie stated things took a turn when Devin got a visit from my mother. We believe your mother must have told him about his father's death, and Devin took it pretty hard. One of the staff training members went in and saw his body inside his bathroom tub. "He must have kept the medication in his mouth prescribed to him every day. When he had enough, he took the medication, went into the bathtub, sat there, and drowned."

"So, my mother came and saw my brother," I stated.

Debbie agreed that she visited the facility and stayed for hours with Devin till visiting time was over. The date Debbie gave me was the day my mother left the note on the kitchen counter. I informed Debbie of the horrible news that my mother had died. She was shocked by the news of what had happened to my mother and was heartbroken. I thanked her for speaking with me, and we ended the call. Then, I picked up the phone and called Pamela and told her to call everyone and instruct them once again to come to the house.

I never knew much about my brother Devin as I drove home and thought about what to do. Not only did I have to lay my mother to rest but also my brother. I tried hard to focus on the road and rush home. However, as the heavy rain hit my windshield and the lightning flashed in the gray clouds, I pictured the heavy rain as my tears. I couldn't shed another tear. I thought, whoever is out to kill my family, I must be next. Once I arrived home, everyone was under the side patio as they waited for me to let them inside. Everyone made it except for Sasha, which I understood, as she was home not feeling well due to her pregnancy. I asked Pamela to warm up some coffee and allow me to put Erickson down for his nap.

"What's going on, Melinda," said Sheldon.

"Tell me that the police found your mother and that she is okay," said Otis Peterson.

As I shook my head, no, the tears I had been waiting for finally came, and I spoke. "She DEAD."

The thunder broke into a roar as the lights began to blink on and off.

"WHAT THE FUCK is going on," stated Tasha.

"Whose ass do I need to beat, cause a bitch like me don't mind going to jail," she said.

The house settled after the thunder and lightning. "That's not all," I stated; as Sheldon rushed to the kitchen, grabbed a napkin, and wiped my face. I sniffed and told them what had happened to Devin.

"On the day she left home, my mother went and saw Devin. I believe she was on her way back home before her death. I don't know what to do, and I have nobody now; what am I to do!" I shouted.

"Melinda, you have us," said Pamela. "We are here for you always."

Having to do two funerals, I decided to do a double ceremony for my mother and brother. They both were buried next to my father, Maxwell. I couldn't believe they were gone as I watched both caskets slowly being lowered to the ground. After the service, I couldn't bear staying home, so Erickson and I agreed to go to the movies. Money had been blowing my phone up, wanting to talk. So, I suggested that she tag along with Erickson and me. Once the movie was over, we prepared to head back home so Money could discuss how she was feeling. We walked to the parking lot. We located my car, and Erickson got in. Then I heard a loud fuss from Money as someone in a black mask tried to rob her in plain sight. The gunman came toward me, demanding that I give up everything I had. Money did all she could to protect me from the robber, but when I heard a loud gunshot, I tried to run and see if Money was okay. Someone from behind pulled me and placed a wet cloth over my face. I struggled, but everything around me went black as my body surrendered, and I went out cold.

I woke up with my hands chained above my head as I screamed for someone to help me. I pleaded for the kidnapper to not hurt me; as I looked around. Everything looked so familiar, and I remembered. It was the same exact place in my dream. The dream I had been having since I was locked up.

"Please, where is my son? Please don't hurt my baby, please. I have money, tell me the amount you need, and I will give it to you. Please let us go. Where is my son?" I screamed.

A familiar voice spoke from the darkness. My eyes grew large as Erick walked toward me.

"Well, well, well, if it isn't my baby fucking mother, Melinda Stone." He came to me with a pistol in hand. "I saved the best for last," he laughed.

"Erick, you- you -you alive?"

"In the flesh, baby," as he slid the pistol on my cheek. "Now, how will you die? It was so easy killing everyone else."

"You killed my parents, but why," I said.

"It wasn't just me; I had some help, baby." Erick placed the gun behind his back.

"Your father, well, I came up with the idea of cutting his brake line."

"Your mother, that loud bitch wouldn't stop screaming, causing a fucking scene. I almost got caught, so we had to stab her ass. How she cried just like you from the pain of every stabbing we did to her precious body. Now your brother did us a favor by taking his own life like a bitch."

I cried so hard hearing what Erick had done to my family.

I took a deep breath and asked what happened to Victoria (aka Kitty), for Otis's sake.

"Your sister- your sister, well, she was trying to mess up my entire scheme. She knew about you with my help, of course. You should be glad I took that bitch out; she's the one that got your brother's mind all fucked up. You see, she is the bitch that dated your brother, but not technically, cause I had to force Kitty, as she was more of a soft bitch. Several times she tried to mess up everything. That final time I had to cut that bitch loose. Kitty was on and off drugs, so I gave her something she'd never forget. Once that bitch smoked that shit in that pipe, Stacey and I took her body, tied a rope around her precious neck, and hung her. Of course, Stacey's idea was to leave a suicide note," laughed Erick.

"Where is my son, you son of a bitch." I screamed.

"Well, he's my son too, and he's never got the chance to meet his daddy. But now he has that chance because I'll be raising him now."

Damn, you are still beautiful. Erick pulled my face to his and kissed me. As the odor of his breath from drinking so much liquor reached my nose, I tried to snatch my head away. Erick ripped my blouse and started kissing my body as he lifted one of my breasts from the cup of my bra and sucked on my nipple. Erick lifted my skirt with the other hand and placed two fingers inside my pussy.

"Mmm, you always stayed wet," he said as he licked my juices from his fingers. Erick went over to a large table. I heard rattling of some sort, and Erick popped something in his mouth and chugged it down with liquor.

"You fucked me up, Melinda. I mean, you really fucked me up," Erick said.

"Erick, I'm sorry I didn't mean to hurt you; please just let me go. I promise not to say a word to anybody that you are alive. Please let me and my son go."

I never thought I would feel the pain of Erick's hand again hitting my face. As I felt the sting of his slap, I tasted the blood on my lips.

"Your family had to pay for my brother's death. He was all I had. Our mother didn't give a fuck about us; we slept anywhere we could lay our fucking heads. You could have tried harder to give him a lesser sentence. I knew about the deal you made and the money they paid you to get my brother to take the max." It was true I was paid to get Silk to take the max, but that was confidential. I was young, and it was my first case. I never told anyone what I had done, not even my father.

So, when I heard the tragic death of Silk on the news, I was devastated at what I had done. True, I could have fought harder, but I never told anybody, as I didn't want my father's company to go down in flames.

"Erick, I'm sorry, please don't do this, please," I cried out.

Erick got up, came behind me, and grabbed a handful of my hair, my neck laid on his shoulder as he grabbed my throat. Again, Erick lifted my skirt, pulled my panties to the side as he unzipped his pants, and hit his dick on my thighs a couple of times. Then I realized what Erick had popped into his mouth was pills. As he whispered into my ears and repeated how bad I fucked him up, Erick pounded several times inside my pussy. The feeling of him inside me disgusted me. Finally, after a few strokes and heavy breathing, Erick exploded. I heard chatting coming nearby as I screamed for someone to help me. Two familiar people approached Erick, and I couldn't believe my eyes. Stacey Washington and Travis Freeman were looking at me.

"Stacey, you knew all this time that Erick was alive, and after everything I did to get you probation, you knew this whole time?"

Stacey chuckled and nodded her head yes. "How can I snitch on my husband's well-being. Saying he wasn't dead?"

"YOUR HUSBAND!" I shouted.

"Yes, my husband." Stacey looked me up and down and saw that I had a ripped blouse and my skirt was wrinkled. She pushed Erick so hard that he almost lost his balance.

"Nigga you fucked her, didn't you?"

"Bitch, if you do that shit one more time," Erick reached for his gun and pointed it at Stacey.

"My mutha fucking ass will become a fucking widow." Stacey backed away from Erick.

"Where is my son," said Erick to Stacey.

"He's fine," she said as she walked back to where Erickson was held hostage in another room. I asked why Travis was here.

"Oh, you didn't know, did you? Travis is my cousin," said Erick.

Travis licked his lips. "Melinda, Melinda, baby girl, I knew you too. You see, I had to put up a front in front of my boys in Costa Rica and Miami. I had to let big cuz know that I was on your fucking trail. I followed you. I'm truly sorry to have to waste a good piece of fine ass," said Travis.

"Damn Melinda, you give anybody the pussy," said Erick.

"Oh, I heard about you and my cousin. How does it feel fucking two relatives?" Erick and Travis fist-bumped one another and laughed.

As my sore arms still hanging above my head, I asked in agony, who shot Money and why? "I did," said Travis, "That bitch had it coming trying to fight me. Your lover had to go."

Money was the one that Miss Cleo informed me about as I cried that everyone I loved was gone and I was next to die. But I had to stay strong and fight for the sake of my son Erickson. As I screamed again for help, Erick informed me that nobody would hear me. The old run-down mill had been abandoned for years, and it was where he and Stacey had been hiding.

***

At the office, Pamela called my phone again to find out if I was okay. After about ten missed calls, she knew something was up. *This isn't like Melinda not showing up for work.* Finally, a knock came on her office door. She answered. Enter! Sheldon walked with Otis Peterson. "I went by the house, and I didn't see Melinda's car. Nobody was home either. So, I came here. Is she here?" Otis asked.

"NO, she's not here, I've been calling her cell, and she hasn't picked up," said Pamela.

"Something is not right. Melinda might be in trouble," said Sheldon.

Pamela logged onto her computer and started typing something; a location appeared on the screen. "Where the fuck is this at?" She murmured.

"What did you find?" Otis asked.

"This may sound crazy, but back in college, Melinda and I used to put tracking devices on any equipment we had to find each other's whereabouts. I located her phone's GPS, which is what it's showing me. But right here is the dead-end of the map. After graduation, we agreed not to go on with this crazy idea and delete all tracking, but I decided to continue." Guilty, Pamela felt terrible about hiding this from Melinda, but she couldn't let Melinda know that she continued to track her. It was how Pamela witnessed the affair Melinda had with Money. "Damn, you and Melinda did some crazy shit in college," joked Sheldon. Pamela gave Sheldon the evil stare, letting him know to be quiet, considering what she and Melinda told him inside her condo.

"Melinda could be in trouble; we should go," stated Otis.

"I don't know. This could be dangerous," said Pamela.

"Let's inform the police."

"We can do that while on the way there. I have to get to my daughter and save her. I couldn't save and protect Victoria. I have a second chance to save Melinda, and if you are too scared to go, then damn it, I'm going alone," shouted Otis.

"Hold on just a second." Pamela went inside her desk and pulled out a box containing two 9mm guns. One belonged to Melinda, the same one that she shot and fired on Stacey and Erick. The other was Pamela's, a gift Maxwell gave to both girls for protection.

"Here, take this, she said.

"Oh no, Otis said. "I don't tolerate guns."

"Fuck it, I'll take it," said Sheldon as he placed the gun behind his back and his tailor suit jacket concealed it.

"Let's go save Melinda!"

While on the road, Pamela called for law enforcement to head out to the GPS address she gave them to locate Melinda. She told one of the police officers on the phone that Melinda was in trouble and for a crime, which sentenced her to five years in prison, a sentence she shouldn't have served. Confused on the other end, the policeman jotted on a pad everything Pamela said but became disconnected as they approached a dead zone.

"Shit, I hope he got everything," Pamela said.

She checked her phone, and there was no signal. Finally, the GPS came to its final spot. The three had to travel and figure out which way to go as they all agreed to keep driving straight until they got to a dead end or found someone for help along the way. As they drove a few more miles down, there was nothing in sight but trees and a couple of old abandoned buildings. Spotting Melinda's car, Pamela told Otis to stop.

"Look, there's Melinda's car! What the fuck, is she doing out here in the middle of nowhere?"

The three parked nearby and walked to see what was happening. Why was Melinda's car at this abandoned mill plant? As they walked a few more steps closer, they heard loud noises that became voices talking inside.

"Let's get a better view," said Sheldon.

"Come back here," demanded Pamela. "We don't know who's in there or where Melinda is."

Sheldon dismissed Pamela. He took off his tailor-made jacket, threw it onto the grass, rolled up his sleeves, and proceeded to walk toward the noise.

***

Stacey came out holding little Erickson's hand. The tears in his eyes showed just how scared he was and wanted his mommy. He cried when he saw Melinda standing up with her hands above her head in chains—he called for Melinda and tried to run to save his mother. As Erickson ran toward Melinda, Erick caught him behind his neck and snatched him up in his arms.

"Hello, son, I'm your daddy."

"Please don't hurt my son," shouted Melinda.

"Shut up bitch, and let me have a conversation with my boy."

Shaken little Erickson greeted Erick but still didn't know who the man was and told Erick, my papa, my daddy; he went away. Erick laughed and apologized to Erickson for losing his grandfather, who raised him as his own son while Melinda was in prison.

"I want my mommy, please, mister, don't hurt my mommy."

Erickson did his best to reach for Melinda and grab her. Erick looked at Melinda, then Erickson, as he struggled to get close to his mother. "This is the only thing I've been waiting on," he held Erickson tighter in his arms.

"Don't hurt him, Erick, please."

"Hurt him bitch. I'm going to raise him, me, and my wife; this is our son now. You will be dead." Melinda screamed so loudly and did all she could to try and release herself from the chains, but it was no use. Her arms were in so much pain from being held up for so many hours that she was too weak to do anything. Erick turned to Stacey.

"Bitch, what the fuck is he doing out here."

Scared, Stacey said he wanted a snack.

"Get him out of my sight," demanded Erick. Travis came rushing down the stairs to let Erick know he had to bounce.

"You don't want to hit that before you go," pointing at me still with the pistol in his hand. "Naw, cuz I got to handle some business," they extended a fist pump.

Travis walked out of the mill, not knowing that Pamela, Sheldon, and Otis were outside. When Travis stepped outside before walking to his car, he lit a blunt. Travis turned and spotted Sheldon coming at him; as he tried to reach for his gun behind his back, Sheldon hit Travis with the end of his pistol. Travis held his face, moaning in pain, wondering how the fuck Sheldon found the spot that Erick and Stacey had been hiding.

"FUCK!" Travis said, still in pain.

"Sheldon, is that you nigga? You want some more of that ass beating I gave you at Monica's crib?"

"Where's Melinda," Sheldon asked, pointing the gun in Travis's face.

"Nigga I'm not telling you shit. I should have killed you when I had the chance for fucking my bitch and getting her ass knocked up."

Travis leaned forward and spitted on Sheldon's custom-made thousand-dollar polish shoes. Sheldon kicked Travis in the face as Pamela ran with the gun unlocked and loaded. Pamela asked Travis again about Melinda's whereabouts. Still, Travis kept his loyalty to his cousin and didn't let them know that Melinda and Erickson were inside. One-shot was fired the bullet hit Travis in the arm as Pamela was tired of the games.

"There's more where that came from," she said.

"Bitch you shot me," yelled Travis.

"And I will do it again if you don't tell me where Melinda is," still pointing the gun at Travis. Travis tried to get up and attack Pamela, but Sheldon stepped in; both men wrestled to the ground, fighting blow for blow.

Travis got ahold of Melinda's gun from Sheldon. Sheldon fought to secure the gun back in his possession. Pamela tried her best to break up the fight, but it was no use; both men were too strong to break apart by herself. However, hearing a shot fired, Pamela didn't want to suspect the worst as both men laid still; a couple of seconds later, Sheldon pushed Travis's dead body off him while Pamela helped him stand to his feet.

Otis came running to see all the commotion as he viewed Travis's body; he bent down to check his pulse and told them Travis was dead.

"Are you two, ok? We need the officials. Take care of one another till I return," said Otis.

They watched Otis drive off to locate help and get the signal back on his phone. Finally, Pamela was ready to go inside, not having a plan; her only thought once entering the building was to save Melinda.
Sheldon grabbed Pamela's hand, kissed her on the lips, and told her to stay behind him as both had their pistols in hand. The smell of rust and water from the pipelines greeted them. Sheldon and Pamela entered and wondered what they would discover.

Hiding behind some barrels, Pamela and Sheldon spotted Melinda chained up to some pipes as a man with his back to them was in front of her. Unfortunately, they couldn't get a view of who the man was. In an angry tone, Melinda asked Erick what the holdup was and why he hadn't killed her yet. Erick reached into his back pocket and pulled out several cards along with a knife. He held the card in her face; Melinda glanced to see that it was her mother's driver's license. Melinda cried and shouted, why my mother.

"I did you a favor; you told me your mother didn't like you as a child and still didn't like you now. You should be happy. I did your ass a favor. Now look at you; both parents are dead, and you get to have everything. But once you're dead, Erickson, your son, I mean our son is the last heir, and he gets everything. I did my research, I got my moneymaker, and I'm rich."

Erick opened up a pocket knife that had the blood of Melinda's mother on the blade. Erick did one cut on Melinda's stomach as Melinda screamed with pain; the blood from her bled a little onto her wrinkled skirt. Then, Erick turned around to place the knife on the table. Pamela's eyes became wide as she knew who the man was. Pamela wanted to scream, but Sheldon placed his hand across her mouth.

"Who is that?" Sheldon whispered.

"That's Erick, and he's alive!"

Stacey came from behind a door with Erickson holding his hand to take him back. Pamela pointed out Stacey to Sheldon and indicated that Stacey knew all along. She had to get a piece of Stacey's lying ass. Without thinking, Pamela got up from her hiding place, screamed Erick's name, and let Melinda go.

Erick turned to face Pamela with a gun in her hand pointed directly at him.
Pamela smirked. "BOY, I will kill you, and this time you will never have to fake your death. I'll make sure you're dead the same way your friend Travis is lying outside on the ground."

"You killed my cousin bitch?"

Not thinking, Erick lifted his gun toward Pamela's face. Both stood staring at each other as they heard a voice.

"No nigga, I did," Sheldon stood up from behind the barrel.

"Well, if it's not bitch ass Sheldon, you fucked my cousin's bitch and got a fucking baby by her whore ass."

Sheldon tilted his head to say, yeah, I did.

Looking Erick straight in the eyes raised his gun, unlocked and loaded-"Let Melinda go, or there'll be bullets flying in this mutha-fucker!"

Melinda SCREAMED No! After hearing Sheldon, she began to beg and plead for Erick to have a heart. Sobbing, Melinda had only one option left and had to use it. Thinking about all that she had lost. If Melinda wanted to save her life and be reunited with her son Erickson, she didn't have a choice.

"If you don't let me go, please, before you kill me, let me make a phone call," Melinda pleaded. "I promise you it's a lot you don't understand. You can even put the call on speaker. Please, Erick, if you are going to kill me, just let me have this one phone call," Melinda begged.

Erick watched out for Pamela and Sheldon and slowly got his phone as Pamela and Sheldon kept their guns drawn on him. Erick dialed the numbers Melinda said to him. The phone rang and clicked. "Hello," a woman answered.

Melinda asked to speak with Christopher Knight. The woman paused and then asked for the private code to be directed to Mr. Knight. Melinda gave it, and her call was directed to be transferred. As they all waited for the call to be transferred, Erick got a little intense, thinking Melinda was setting him up. But he waited to see where this was all going. Then, finally, a click happened on the line, Melinda, hearing the click pleaded....

"I can't hold this any longer. It's time!! I'm with Erick, and he has me, hostage," Melinda shouted.

Erick was about to end the call when he heard a familiar raspy voice, "Hey, Bro. It's me, Silk...."

Words from the Author

I am Charlene, the daughter of Althea and the late Charles Workman Sr. I was born in Georgia, a homeschool diploma graduate from Faith Academy. I was diagnosed with scoliosis, which caused me to become paralyzed at an early age. But with the support and prayers from family and friends, God wasn't ready to give up on my story. By faith and with dedication and hard work, I began to walk again with the help of the Shepherd center.

I'm surprised to say I never thought becoming an author would bring my name into the spotlight as my passion for music and writing my own music, I thought, would take off once I moved to Atlanta, Ga. My future goals, of course, is writing more books and being with my three beautiful children. Hopefully, one day, I look forward to traveling and enjoying what my heavenly father has for me, the many more blessings waiting daily for my life...

For my readers, thank you for taking the time to read my first novel. I hope it brings you excitement, love, laughter, and some tears, as it has been for me while writing it...

With all my love,

Charlene Workman